Beyond Gates

Talia Arabiat

Copyright ©2024 Talia Arabiat

All rights reserved.

"Beyond Gates," published through Young Author Academy.

Young Author Academy FZCO

Dubai, United Arab Emirates

www.youngauthoracademy.com

ISBN: 9798884177130

Printed by Amazon Direct Publishing.

ACKNOWLEDGEMENTS

I want to thank my family for their unwavering support, especially Mom, who kept reminding me to write when I felt the most discouraged. Without your unconditional support, I would still be on page 1.

I would also like to thank my English teachers at my current school; I wouldn't have come this far without your consistent guidance (and reminder to vary my sentence lengths)!

Thank you to my friends, who had no idea I was writing a book but gave me inspiration nonetheless.

And last but not least, I want to thank J.K. Rowling, Chris Colfer, and Julie C. Dao for inspiring me to write a book of my own.

Table of Contents

- Prologue -

Hidden far from sight, amid overgrown bushes and brambles, an enchanted door as old as time stood regally. Only those with magic in their blood are permitted to enter the majestic lands that lay beyond it. And, though unaware in the moment, the first person who does manage to break the magical seal of the door will change the world as we know it today.

- Chapter 1 -

Warning in Disguise

Thirteen-year-old Courtney Carter woke up with a start. It was the seventh night in a row she awoke to the same nightmare - and it was starting to get on her nerves now.

***

It started with her best friend, Katie Clover's party, which was located in a mysterious yet captivating garden.

Surrounding the area was a breathtaking sea of lush greenery. Glorious golden pothos and long vines of philodendron were swaying in the light breeze, and sun rays peeked in from between the branches of enormous fern trees.

Courtney entered the party gracefully with her mother and elder sister, looking around in awe. Courtney greeted Katie's mother with a warm smile, then went off to join her friends.

Time flew by until she suddenly spotted a vast wooden door out of the corner of her eye. The door was so engulfed in different plants of all species, that it was practically hidden. She pointed this out to Katie, but Katie only laughed and changed the subject.

After Courtney pointed the door out for the third time to Katie, all her friends vanished into thin air. The door slowly opened, and a hissing sound emitted from the opening in the void of the doorway as smoke slowly filled the air around her.

A high, cold voice rang in Courtney's ears, "You cannot help others if you cannot help yourself, and if you cannot help yourself, you won't be able to save your loved ones from the tragedies that are coming their way. Before it's too late...

everything depends on you."

After a week of dreaming the same dream, she realised it wasn't just a nightmare... it was a message.

"Courtney," Mrs. Carter called, "come down for breakfast!"

Courtney immediately snapped out of her trance and leisurely climbed down the steps leading to the kitchen, where her mother had prepared a stack of pancakes topped with fresh berries for her.

"Where's Amelia?" Courtney enquired as she took her first bite. "I thought she had a quiz competition today."

"She does," her mother replied, shooting a glance at the clock, "but it starts at midnight, so she's sleeping in today."

Courtney's big sister, Amelia, was naturally gifted at science and had won countless medals for her outstanding performance in competitions.

"Thanks for the breakfast, Mum," Courtney said and rushed upstairs to her room.

What did 'help yourself' really mean? And what 'tragedies' was the disembodied voice trying to warn her about? When was 'too late' and why is she the one who has to save the others?

Courtney had so many questions, and there was nobody she could ask. If she told her mother, she would check if Courtney was experiencing a fever. If she asked her sister, she would laugh and tell Courtney to get out of her room in case her craziness was contagious.

Courtney felt all alone. Alone, and in need of answers as soon as possible. Just one week ago, her biggest concern was her upcoming history examination, which she took with the grumpiest, surliest, sourest teacher in the school.

But the idea of worrying about her history teacher and exams when her choices could be the only difference between life and death for everyone, she knew was laughable. She was going to help herself -whatever that meant- and help her loved ones. She just needed a little help... but from whom?

She sat on her desk and pondered the matter until her head hurt. What if it was just a dream?

No, she can't have the same dream seven nights in a row, it must be a warning. But who was trying to warn her? And couldn't they have been a bit clearer when telling Courtney about the tragedies everyone would have to face if she didn't help herself in time to help them?

Courtney was just a thirteen-year-old, after all. Could she do this?

Courtney had always been an optimist, but what bright side was there to view? She began thinking of the good qualities she possessed that could help in her search for answers. She was an intelligent girl; she could figure anything out. She had brilliant blue eyes that could see from miles away and impeccable hearing, which could help her if she needed to look for something in order to 'help herself'.

Most importantly, she had the bravery, courage and confidence of her whole family combined. She could solve anything, and she knew she could save her friends, family, and possibly the whole world if she put her mind to it. She just needed time, but she didn't have much left.

Courtney had to make a plan, and quickly. She recalled, as best as she could remember, the words she heard coming from the other side of the door in her dream. Then she described the setting that the scene from her dream took place in and the strange door, the door that opened to endless possibilities.

Then Courtney remembered that her mother once took a tour of the country; she knew every part of their city like the back of her hand. She excitedly rushed down the stairs to the kitchen and sat down at the counter just like she did when she was a little girl.

"Mum?" she spoke.

Mrs. Carter was extremely busy; she was rushing from the refrigerator to the cupboard, sink to stove, then accidentally dropped a large bag of flour on the just-polished marble floor. Coughing uncontrollably, she emerged from the cloud of white powder looking like she just walked out of a blizzard.

"Yes?" she spluttered.

Courtney realised it might not have been the perfect time to start a conversation like this when her mother was so stressed. "Never mind, you seem busy, it can wait," Courtney replied.

She didn't want to be the reason another disaster happened while her mother talked to her. "What are you doing, anyways? You look like you did when Mr. and Mrs. Queen were coming for dinner, but from the message, you thought the actual queen was coming here," she teased.

"Very funny," Mrs. Carter snapped, "this is for your sister, she has a competition tonight. Now go up to your room and let me clean up this mess."

Laughing hysterically, Courtney left, thinking about the amount of food there would be on the table when Amelia woke up. She went up to her room, where she decided to lie down for a while.

"Where's mum?" a groggy voice asked from Courtney's doorway.

Without looking up, Courtney replied, "Morning, Amelia, mum's downstairs making you breakfast, she says you need a 'big energy boost' for tonight, so there'll be a plate of pancakes stacked to the ceiling waiting for you in the kitchen."

Amelia groaned and Courtney smirked. Amelia hated it when her mother would 'go to unnecessary extremes' because of her contests. "I've been going to these quiz competitions since I was fi-pancakes, you say? I don't mind too much this time then," she laughed.

"Why don't you change first?" Courtney teased, eyeing her fifteen-year-old sister's worn-out robe and the rollers tangled in her thick strawberry-blonde tresses.

Amelia rolled her eyes and left the room, leaving Courtney alone with her questions. However, she was thankful for the short distraction, it helped her think clearly. She was slowly starting to understand how to help herself. The key was not to worry too much, it was about finding a balance.

And to get her answers, she would need to find that door.

- Chapter 2 -

Setting Off

A flashlight. A bag filled with fruits, sandwiches, and snacks. Bottled water. A pocket knife. A small pouch of saved pocket money. A change of clothes.

Courtney was embarking on a journey - possibly the biggest journey of her life - and she was preparing for it by putting all of the things she needed in a large backpack. Oh, and she almost forgot, she needed a first-aid kit.

Once Courtney double and triple-checked that she had everything she needed, she hid her backpack in her room and came back down for a second breakfast with Mum and Amelia. She usually didn't like to have breakfast twice, but

- just like her sister - she always made an exception for pancakes.

Amelia sighed, "Mum, this is happening every time, you're doing too much for me. It must stop. I have a competition, not dinner with the queen."

A giggle escaped Courtney, and she was shot a dirty look by Mrs. Carter. "I'm not doing too much!" she replied, "I'm just making sure you have enough energy for your competition. I would be a careless mother if I didn't feed you well, today of all days."

Amelia didn't know what to say, so there was a moment of silence until Courtney broke it.

"Mum, I made plans with friends for today and tomorrow, and Katie said I could sleep over at the Clovers, can I go?" she lied. Whatever the answer, she would still sneak out. She just wanted an excuse if it was possible.

"Next time, you ask your mother before you make plans with your friends, young lady. Well, you can't cancel on them now, so I suppose you could go. But just this once," she replied sternly.

"Thanks!" Courtney said, shoving another syrupy mouthful of pancakes into her mouth. Then she took the silence that followed as an opportunity to ask her mother what she couldn't before. "Remember when you went on that tour of the country?" she asked her mother, trying her best to sound simply curious and not like she was gathering as much information as possible to set out on a journey to hunt for a door she didn't have proof existed.

Mrs. Carter nodded. "What about it?" she curiously asked.

"Well, I have an upcoming geography test, and I thought you could help me a little, seeing as you have better knowledge of this country than all my geography teachers combined," Courtney joked.

Her mother, surprised at her daughter's sudden interest in geography as she usually despised the subject, sensed something fishy was going on.

Geography? Same-day plans for sleeping over at a friend's place? Even the large droopy bags under Courtney's eyes seemed out of character for the sleep addict.

Mrs. Carter knew what was going on, but she didn't dare reveal her suspicions. She hid her chuckle behind a napkin.

"Alright then. What do you want to know about? Map symbols? Navigation skills practice? Grid references? Contour lines?" Mrs. Carter asked, pretending not to know.

"Actually, I was hoping for something a bit more specific," Courtney retaliated, "what do you know about all the parks and gardens in the country?" She was trying her best not to sound too specific, otherwise, it would seem obvious that she wasn't studying for an examination.

"Well, we don't have many gardens or parks, but we do have a few like PetPark, Green Valley Garden, Grow Garden, Greenlia Public Park, Bliss

Park, Fit Flora, Willow Garden, Violet Valley, and Emerald Park," Courtney's Mum replied. "But you know them all, why do you ask?" she added, sounding mildly curious.

"Just revision, in case I forgot something," she blurted, feeling quite stupid because she hadn't thought of an answer in case Mum asked her that question. Her mother could see straight through her lies.

Courtney was desperate now. What if the door she was looking for was in another country-or didn't even exist? Would Courtney still be able to help herself and the others? She knew this wouldn't be an easy trip, but it was getting harder and harder, and she didn't even start her voyage for the hidden door that opened to more questions and mysteries. That would be hard enough.

She would now have to find the door on her own. She picked up her bag and headed towards the front door.

"See you!" Courtney called to her mother and sister, not knowing when she would see them again.

"Be home by dinner tomorrow!" Mrs. Carter called out as Courtney shut the door behind her.

Courtney might not have known when or even if she would return, but she knew one thing: she would definitely not be home by dinner the next day.

She took a deep breath and stepped out into the world, a soft breeze playing across her face, the wind blowing her strawberry blonde hair backward. She put on her most determined face and took her first step, her journey had officially begun.

Everywhere around her, cars were beeping and trucks were honking. People were walking about, off on their daily errands. Courtney felt foolish being the only one with somewhere to go but not knowing where she was headed.

Where should she start? What would her mum say when she finds out where she really was?

What was she thinking? She couldn't just skip school and set off on her own. What if she got lost? Or kidnapped?

She groaned in a way her history teacher would be proud of. She couldn't go home now, she couldn't actually sleep over at Katie's, and she couldn't spend the night on the streets, so she decided to start by looking around the parks and gardens she was familiar with, hoping the door would be around there. Perhaps she might have overlooked it the hundred or so times she had visited in the past. She sighed an impressively long sigh, then put her determined face back on and headed towards Bliss Park, which was nearest to where she was standing.

Bliss Park was the park closest to Courtney, it was also the one she grew up in. When she was three, she used to visit there every day with a seven-year-old Amelia. When Amelia turned ten, she became so immersed in reading, science and studying that she didn't enjoy playing with Courtney as much as she did before. Courtney smiled bittersweetly. She wished she could have a Harry Potter time-turner of her own to use and to revisit the old days when not a care was on her mind.

Distracted from finding the door, Courtney became excited upon seeing her childhood favourite place in front of her eyes. She giggled and rushed over to the swing she and Amelia used to take turns pushing the other on. She felt a wave of happiness as soon as she took off into the air, and all thoughts of her journey and the mysterious door were erased from her mind. All she could think about were the childhood memories that lay before her. Without realising it, she was slowly starting to help herself.

Time flew by quickly as Courtney was enjoying herself more than she had in a long time. She felt like a little girl again - she just wished Amelia could be there to enjoy it with her. Suddenly, she gasped, remembering why she was there in the first place. She felt embarrassed to have let herself get distracted so easily. She was there on a mission; she had to fulfil it. Not knowing what to expect or what to look out for, she started to walk around the garden slowly, looking at trees, peering into hedges, and gazing at plants like she was inspecting a house for sale. After her third or fourth time circling the park, she had to accept defeat and face the fact that the gate wasn't hiding in this park.

The next-closest garden to Bliss Park was Green Valley Garden, though Courtney doubted that she would find the door there, as the door looked old and withered in her dream, as though it had been around for at least a century, and Green Valley Garden was a smaller, very modern take on Phoenix garden, complete with a brand-new slide and swing set. But she didn't know for sure, so she took a deep breath and stepped inside the wrought iron gate that led to a flower field. The delicate aroma of roses, daisies, and petunias overtook Courtney's senses.

She started collecting a bunch of the most exquisite flowers she could find, and she emerged from the field with a prodigious bouquet of red, blue, purple, white, and pink flowers. Again, she was unknowingly helping herself, a little at a time.

Careful not to lose herself in all the fun once more, Courtney reminded herself that she was thirteen, and thirteen-year-olds don't play in little kids' playgrounds. She took fewer rounds around this garden than she did Bliss Park, and wasn't very surprised when she saw that the gate wasn't lurking in the shadows of the hanging begonias there. She would have to move on.

The next park, Greenlia, wasn't very close by so Courtney chose to rest for a few minutes before setting out again. She sat down on a bench located near the side of the street and watched the cars pass by. She was a very strong-willed girl with a good heart; ready to risk everything to help people the second she thinks they might be in danger. As much as she would like to sit around all day, doing nothing for the rest of the afternoon, she had to get up and about again.

The sooner she found the door, the better, as she didn't know how much time she would spend behind it. Her poor mother was so stressed about Amelia's competition, and when Courtney didn't return home the next day she would be worried sick.

What if she talks to Mrs. Clover? Should Courtney make up a lie? Or should she just come clean and tell the truth?

Courtney decided not to worry about that now. She had a long journey ahead of her, and she figured she could think about everything else later. Right now, she had to get to Greenlia.

She found a discarded map on the floor, a slightly crumpled-up map with ripped corners. It looked ancient. Courtney figured that whoever left the map lying around had left it because of the condition it was in. However, to her, it was like finding buried treasure. It was almost as if someone had known she would need it and had intentionally left it behind to help her...

'No,' Courtney thought firmly. 'I'm doing this completely on my own. Nobody knows about this but me.'

She used a pen she found in her pocket to trace her route from Green Valley Garden to Greenlia Public Park, as it was the closest to where she was and used it to navigate her path.

After around fifteen minutes of walking, Courtney saw a lot of traffic; joggers were huddled together on the sidewalk and cars were jam-packed on the streets. The sound of honking, beeping, tooting, and yelling filled the streets. Courtney couldn't see in front of her or behind her. She was stuck among a big group of runners who were trying to push themselves forward.

"Um, excuse me?" she cautiously asked one of them, a man around her mother's age wearing a blue gym shirt with a matching headband. "Do you have any idea what's going on? I was on my way to Greenlia Public Park when I got caught up in this traffic."

He turned to face her. "There's a lot of construction happening on this road. If you're headed to Greenlia, I suggest you take this path," he said, pointing to a winding road on the opposite side of where they were standing.

"Thank you very much!" Courtney thanked the man, but her smile faltered when she noticed how long the path was, and how much time it would take her to reach. But she was fuelled by adrenaline and was determined to get past that door no matter what it took. Besides, what would a few extra minutes of walking do?

But what Courtney didn't realise was that it wasn't just a few extra minutes of walking, but a couple of days' worth.

- Chapter 3 -

Missing Something

"Amelia, hurry up!" Mrs. Carter called.

Amelia grunted.

"Mum, it's nine-thirty," she said, "I still have plenty of time to revise, the quiz competition starts at twelve."

Mrs. Carter checked her watch. "Minus thirty-minutes to get there, and being early doesn't hurt. You have exactly ninety minutes to revise and get ready."

A sigh of satisfaction escaped Amelia's lips. This was the first time she could revise for her competition without interruptions - such as Courtney's music (which she liked to play at full volume), Courtney babbling on the phone right outside of Amelia's bedroom, or Courtney banging on her door, asking for pencils and scrap pieces of paper - and she was loving it so far.

But there was one thing missing...

Courtney had always accompanied Amelia and her mother to every quiz competition. This time, Amelia couldn't understand why Courtney decided to make plans with her friends on the day of her contest. Not that it mattered that much, but it was just... weird.

Usually, Courtney would love nothing more than to cheer her sister on. Amelia remembered when the eight-year-old version of her sister would sit on one of the benches and hold up a sign that read 'GO AMELIA!'.

Amelia missed the young, energetic Courtney, and though she wouldn't admit it, she secretly wished her sister would become more like her old, clumsy, playful, mischievous self.

"Focus, Amelia, you promised yourself; no distractions," she muttered under her breath.

Amelia's competition started in two hours, and she couldn't lose today. She always won, except for the time when she traded her silver medal for a unicorn pen. She was five, and the pen had little purple hearts on it, what soon-to-be six-year-old could resist that?

But now, she was fifteen. A smart and well-educated young lady. Her trivia competitions were becoming more and more important every time, and this one was no exception. This was the sorting; the competition that determined who was moving to the finals. She had to win this one. But when she settled down to finally do her revision, she felt that something was missing - and this time, it wasn't silence, but the lack of it.

She didn't know why, but the fact that Courtney would prefer sitting with her friends over watching her compete with worldwide science achievers slightly annoyed her. She knew she was being selfish, but one of their family rules was to always be there for each other. The two sisters always have - up until now. Also, Courtney wasn't the type of person who would spend all her time at the mall with friends, talking about make-up and other nonsense while drinking iced coffees. She was the type who loved to sleep in on Sundays and spend the entire day reading books in her grumpy cat pyjamas.

With difficulty, Amelia returned her focus to the textbook in front of her. Nothing was more important than the book sitting on her desk, and it deserved her full attention. Courtney and everything else would have to wait.

"Amelia, are you ready?" Mrs. Carter appeared at the door of Amelia's bedroom one hour later.

Amelia sighed. "Why the long face?" Her mother was surprised to see her so unenthusiastic. "I thought you were excited; today is the sorting!" But Amelia's expression remained stoic. Mrs. Carter knew something was bothering her. "What's wrong?" she asked, sitting down on the bed beside her daughter.

Amelia didn't know what to say. "Never mind,

let's just go, you wanted to be early." She abruptly stood up, and for what seemed like the millionth time that day, Mrs. Carter checked her watch.

"We'll talk in the car, but now let's just go," she said. It wasn't that she didn't want to know what was making her daughter feel so upset, but she always liked to make a good first impression by arriving half an hour early at the very least. She grabbed the car keys, and within minutes, they were off.

"So, do you want to tell me why you're so upset?" Mrs. Carter asked Amelia.

"I-It's nothing," she replied, staring out of the window. "I'm just tired, that's all," she lied, though she wasn't a good liar and her mother knew something was troubling her.

"Amelia, you and I both know very well that-"

"Fine, I'll tell you, but after the competition, alright? Because I don't want anything to distract me now," Amelia interrupted. She just wanted an excuse to stop thinking about Courtney and focus mainly on science.

Her mother agreed, and a heavy silence followed. Mrs. Carter turned on the radio, and time flew by quickly after that. Once they got there, Amelia was introduced to the other contestants, (who apparently, just like Mrs. Carter, loved being early) and given a bottle of water. Half an hour later, the competition began, and Amelia was trying her best to answer every question correctly. Two more rounds were to follow this one, and then a handful of people would be picked for the finals. Mrs. Carter silently said a prayer for Amelia's success. She knew how much this meant to her.

She also wanted Amelia to focus on her competition and not worry about anything else, because Amelia was expecting Courtney to come back home the next day. The only people who knew that she wasn't coming home soon were Courtney herself and, though the thirteen-year-old didn't know it yet, Mrs. Carter. Amelia would worry then, so her mother wanted her to clear her mind today and concentrate on the two things she loved most: science and trivia competitions.

Noticing how calm and clever Amelia was, her contestants rushed and answered with the first things that came into their minds, giving her more of a head start. She smiled at her mother. Mrs. Carter smiled back. Amelia was happy now and knew that Courtney would be happy when she found out how good she was at answering the trivia questions. Amelia just wished her sister was around to see her now, winning the competition - as usual.

- Chapter 4 -

Distracted

Courtney used the map to navigate her path to Greenlia Public Park, and seeing the long path on it again didn't discourage her; in fact, it only reminded her that she had a long journey ahead of her and that she should start if she was going to reach before the end of the week.

People stared at her as they passed her by but she knew that to reach the garden as soon as possible, she needed to just ignore them. Granted, it wasn't every day a thirteen-year-old ventured into the middle of the streets all by herself. And this was no walk to the supermarket.

Courtney walked. And she walked. Then she walked some more. Her breaths were becoming shorter, and her legs slower. She wiped the sweat off her forehead and continued walking. She was determined, and even if the door wasn't in Greenlia, she would walk to the end of the world, and wouldn't be completely satisfied until she was one hundred percent sure that her friends and family would be alright. She just prayed she wouldn't need to walk to the other side of the world because the straps of her backpack were digging into her shoulders and she was panting uncontrollably. Yes, she very much hoped the gate would show itself amongst the trees and bushes of Greenlia Public Park because, despite her excitement to ensure helping others as a priority, she was just a human being, not a robot. And, unlike robots, she could get tired easily.

Courtney needed to stop. And rest. She had never been so tired, hungry, and in need of a shower before like she did now. She would have to take a bus to Greenlia, as she hadn't even covered much land compared to the trail ahead of her. It would do her no good to keep walking.

According to the map, the next bus stop was a couple of minutes walking distance away, and Courtney had to drag her legs forward to reach it. She sat on the bus stop bench as she waited for the bus to Sunshine Street, and she would walk the five minutes to Greenlia Public Park from there.

Courtney sat down and exhaled deeply. She wished she could lie down on the bus stop bench. Why was she so determined to walk to the end of the city and back? Couldn't she have asked her mother or Mrs. Clover to drive her there? She couldn't turn back now. She knew her father would be proud of her if she managed to complete the task ahead of her. He was a very strong-willed person, a trait Courtney had definitely inherited. She was still determined to help others.

Exhaustedly determined.

"Six pounds, please," the lady at the ticket counter said. Courtney hadn't expected the bus ride to be so expensive. She emptied most of her money pouch on the counter. The lady swiped them into the money box and handed Courtney her ticket. Courtney thanked her and waited for her bus to arrive.

It wasn't easy being a thirteen-year-old and running away from home. She would never take her bed for granted again. Stars were scattered across the sky, and a full moon beamed down at her. She would usually be asleep by this time. Then she remembered. According to her watch, it was already past midnight. She had missed the competition. It was the first time Courtney hadn't accompanied her sister for moral support - and for that, she felt devastated.

She wished she could just inform her sister about her whole quest so Amelia didn't think Courtney didn't want to watch her competition because that was definitely not true. Courtney would love nothing more than to go to her sister's trivia competition at this very moment. It was just that, as much as she wanted to see her sister crush her contestants, this was far more important.

The overhead speakers announced that the bus to Sunshine Street station would be departing in ten minutes and that boarding was now open.

Courtney gathered her belongings and stood up, but was immediately swept off her feet by the huge crowd of people trying to get to the bus.

After five confusing minutes of being constantly pushed around, Courtney found her way to the bus. She quickly claimed the last seat before anyone could take it. Never before was she this tired or in need of a nap. Before she knew it, her head was resting on her shoulder and her eyelids were slowly closing over her eyes. In her dazed and frequent dreams, the door kept popping up, reminding her that she was getting closer to the 'too late' she was warned against.

Courtney slept for the next two hours on the bus, but when the automatic doors opened and a bell rang, she abruptly woke up and yawned. Her sleep may have been uncomfortable and filled with nightmares, but she was still grateful for any rest she could get.

One by one, the passengers dismounted the bus. Courtney was the last and most unenthusiastic person to exit. Not finding the gate in Greenlia Public Park only meant more walking, and her knees already felt like jelly as she climbed the steps down from the bus.

Courtney took out her map once more. She needn't walk long from there, for Greenlia Public Park was a five-minute walk away. The two-hour nap she took on the bus was enough to re-energise her and get ready to explore again, although she didn't feel like it. But did she really have a choice?

She shivered and secretly wished she had brought a jacket along. But instead of stopping, she ran as fast as she could. She figured, the sooner she found the gate, the better. When Courtney began to get stitches in her side, she decided to slow down a little. But there was no need; a large wooden arrow that read 'GREENLIA PUBLIC PARK' pointed to a park on Courtney's left. Calling Greenlia 'big' was an understatement. It was a colossal, magnificent green esplanade with perfectly manicured rose bushes.

Small sandpits were scattered around amongst the grassy lawns, and the finest slides, swings, and seesaws were available for the children's pleasure.

They almost looked too good to be used.

Suddenly, out of nowhere, a marching band dressed in red and white appeared, followed by a parade. There were carriages, unicycles, trains, dancers, and many more forms of entertainment. Courtney had to admit, the performance was pretty captivating. She couldn't help but dance along, and soon enough, she was twirling, tap dancing, and laughing along to the instrumental music.

Pink-faced, she reached into her backpack and took a sip of water. Then she reminded herself that the door wasn't going to find itself and that dancing and messing around wouldn't help her whatsoever. Little did she know, however, that it was helping her - it was helping more than it would to look around this park.

Courtney pretended to examine the rose bushes so as not to look suspicious, even though she was actually looking for the gate. But there was no need for that, as all eyes were wrapped around the parade, and nobody seemed to notice her, let alone be suspicious of her.

The park was far too large to be looked around more than once, so Courtney wasn't hesitant to move on after turning every leaf and inspecting every bush, only to discover that the door wasn't there, either.

She looked back at her map which was her sole guiding light in this ever-frustrating Quest. PetPark was one hour's walking distance away, but it was very late now, and despite her two-hour snooze, Courtney was still very tired. She decided to turn in for the night.

While exiting the park, Courtney tried to think of places where she could rest. She didn't have enough money to pay for a hotel, and that was pretty much the only place she could sleep outside of home. She hadn't considered what she was going to do about her sleeping situation before this.

She had no option but to rest outdoors. The only place where she could have a seat was a bench on the sidewalk similar to the one she sat on before setting off with Greenlia as her destination. She sighed. This was harder than she thought it was going to be, but she knew giving up was not an option.

Because she knew deep inside that she was doing this for herself just as much as she was doing it for her family and friends.

Courtney gazed at the stars and wondered what made her so sure that she was meant to be there all along. And she didn't find an exact answer. But that was fine - she didn't have to have a justified explanation for everything. She just trusted her instinct, and if it brought her here, then that was where she was meant to be. Why else would she have gotten these dreams, if not for a good purpose?

Courtney sat down and sighed. She planned her journey the next day. She would wake up bright and early, then walk the one hour to PetPark. Closest to PetPark was Violet Valley, which was a few hour's walk away. But now, all that mattered was the sleep she was yearning for since the second she had woken up.

Courtney used her bag as a pillow, and despite how uncomfortable it was, she fell asleep the instant her head touched it. Disturbing images cropped up in her dreams, of her family and friends in trouble, of her mother and sister worrying over her mysterious disappearances, of the disembodied voice reminding her of her failure, and of how disappointed everyone would be of her if she didn't manage to find the gate.

She wondered what her mother and sister were doing. She hoped they weren't too worried about her. After all, she is independent and able to manage on her own... right?

She kept waking up in a cold sweat and then, taking a deep breath, she would go back to sleep. It was inarguably the worst night of her life, but she didn't complain. As long as she was doing this for the people she loved, it was worth it. She just wished someone would be there to accompany her. It was a lonely quest. But that was how it was supposed to be. Courtney and Courtney only.

The noise of cars on the street didn't bother her. Being on the run for more than a day made her accustomed to loud noises and large crowds, so the sound was quite soothing to Courtney now.

She must have slept for quite a while because the last things she saw before her eyes closed were the twinkling stars and the full moon, and the first thing she saw when she opened her eyes was the sun beaming brightly and singing birds gliding from one evergreen tree to the next. It was such a beautiful day.

Courtney wouldn't have loved anything more than to stay on that bench all day, but she knew that she had a job ahead of her and that she should finish it.

PetPark was her next destination. The shortest time possible to reach there was an hour. And she would reach there within forty-five minutes. It wasn't a question, but a statement. Because if she could do this, she could do anything.

She slung her backpack over her shoulder and bounced off the bench, ready to start a new day with a positive note. Courtney didn't walk or jog; she was now running like her life depended on it. Clutching a stitch in her side, she panted harder than she ever did in her life, but she didn't stop. She couldn't stop. The time flew by and her blonde ponytail swung from side to side as she ran.

Forty-five minutes later, she heard a series of barking, meowing, chirping, and squeaking. She had arrived at her destination, a wheezing mass of sweaty gym clothes and sparkly purple sneakers.

All around her, pets of all sizes and species mingled with each other. From huge English Mastiffs to tiny Singapura cats, the park lived up to its name and more. This was the perfect place to treat and pamper your pet. Courtney was enthralled... until she stepped in a pile of excrement - and had no idea where that came from.

She gasped and laughed as pets all around her began running, chasing each other, and scarfing down the pet food left for them in their designated areas.

Bending down to pet them, she forgot the whole reason she was there. Being surrounded by so much happiness helped her - she was helping herself more and more, but not in the way she thought she would...

Courtney closed her eyes and massaged her forehead - Why was she always getting distracted? If it's not swinging or arranging flowers, then it's dancing or playing around with distracting - but completely adorable - furry fellows.

She had forgotten, once again, why she was there today. If she didn't hunt for the gate, nobody would. She had to get going - meow.

- Chapter 5 -

Lost

Unsurprisingly, Courtney didn't find what she was looking for in PetPark. She didn't expect to but it was discouraging nonetheless. Her next destination was Violet Valley, as it was the park closest to her.

It was a long walk, but Courtney managed to gather up her strength and carry on. But there was only one thing she left behind - her optimism.

She dragged her feet like they were encased in concrete, walking like a zombie on the path that would lead her to Violet Valley (according to the map). Her head filled with doubts; what if the door wasn't in any of the parks or gardens she had arranged to visit? Would all her walking, running, and jogging be nothing but a waste of time and worry (on her mother's part)?

Shaking off her doubts and worries, Courtney began to walk a little faster, her heart beating a little more frequently. Even if the parks she listed did not hide the gate in their shadows, at the end of the day she wouldn't have any doubts or haunting questions like if or had, because the only thing worse than failing is not trying at all.

Within the coming couple of hours, after Courtney finally found the magnificent gate she had been desperately hoping to find. The gate welcomed visitors into Violet Valley with open arms, its polished maple wood glinting in the light of the late evening sun, its gleaming brass hinges and handle gleaming.

It was worth walking all the way there just to see the clumps and bushes of violets carefully grown and cared for just inside the gates. Courtney looked around and immediately fell in love with the place.

Conscious of what she came here to do, she began looking for the wooden and withered door, which was an easier task than she expected it to be. Aside from all the grandeur, Violet Valley was not as vast as she had imagined it to be, therefore making her job much easier.

However, after she searched the entire park - twice - she came to the conclusion that she wouldn't find what she sought in that particular place.

But she had done what she came to do, look for the magical door in this garden - would it hurt to have a little fun?

She wouldn't stay for long, it was just that running barefoot into completely violet-endorsed meadows was so tempting. As if in slow motion, Courtney ran towards the violet valleys with her arms outstretched. The sweet scent of the flowers was almost hypnotising as the soft petals brushed her face. She took a deep breath and grinned from ear to ear. Nobody said this trip had to be entirely tiring and boring - she could have a little fun, couldn't she?

She sprawled down on the grassy violet meadows and looked up at the sky as if she was trying to make a snow angel in the dirt. Her next destination was Fit Flora, which was a very sporty park, kind of like an outdoor gym. It was right next to Violet Valley on her map.

Courtney had only been there three times; twice with Mum and Amelia, and once with Katie. As she planned the next part of her thrilling journey, she couldn't help but notice how brilliantly blue the sky was - just like her eyes. And Amelia's, too. But thinking about Amelia and Mum was painful.

Fit Flora was only twenty minutes away from where Courtney was now. But there was only one problem...

Courtney couldn't get up! She had sunk so deep into the violet fields that she wasn't getting up -

not because she didn't want to, but because she couldn't! It took her around five minutes just to get up and about again, and another ten minutes to find her way out of the violet-covered grassland.

Breathing heavily, Courtney quickly checked her map again and, with a confident nod, set off towards Fit Flora. But it wasn't that weird how she went from being completely negative to incredibly confident... She was helping herself in the Violet Valley.

She practically jogged to Fit Flora - being on the run for some time has made her excited to check out the next park, and then the next. Now, it wasn't a long, boring walk from park to park all alone, but an exciting quest that could change her life forever... accompanied by her optimism.

The last time Courtney was out of the house all by herself, it was only for a few hours, and she had a curfew. Now, she could go anywhere she desired, and stay up as long as she liked. And, the best thing about it was that her mum couldn't get mad when she found out - Courtney was doing this for her.

She smirked and carried on with her speed-walking. Before she knew it, she was standing on a paved running track, and all around her was a set of high-tech gym equipment. Courts for every outdoor sport imaginable were facing each other in rows; it was a great place for sports enthusiasts.

Courtney wasn't very sporty, but she couldn't resist trying one of the expensive and high-quality treadmills that stood lined next to each other. Besides, that way, she would be preparing herself for the next trip ahead by warming up.

At first, she started at the 'slow' setting. But after she got used to it a little, she moved on to 'intermediate'. Just as expected, Courtney lost track of time.

Again.

She checked her watch thirty minutes later, and instead of getting huffy or contemplating why she never remembered why she ended up in a certain place, so she decided to solve her problem. She set up a timer on her watch for five minutes. When she would walk into the park, she would press 'start', then complete the necessary tasks. If she ended up distracted (as she would usually be), the alarm would remind her. It was foolproof!

She tried to think how the people who moved all that equipment into the park might have missed the door. But, after all, it was just a gate, and Courtney was possibly the only person alive to know how magical or dangerous the lands beyond it may be. But she was already there – so why not try?

She spent an hour searching and then left. That was ninety minutes wasted in Fit Flora. A park Courtney had always liked was Emerald Park, but she didn't get to visit it much growing up as it wasn't exactly close to home, and her mother didn't feel the need to drive all the way there.

"You could go to Bliss Park," she would always say.

The last time Courtney had been to Emerald Park was on Katie's birthday four years ago, so she was pretty excited to revisit there. Even the fact that the park was almost two hours away didn't bother her. She just kept walking. Nothing could distract her now.

She walked past the science clubs where Amelia would go every day, gyms that her mother used to visit, then quit after two weeks - she even passed Katie's apartment without stopping. Well, she stopped once, but that was only to check her map and carry on. And her walk continued.

Strangely, a red mailbox kept appearing over and over again. Courtney could have sworn the same one at least four times earlier... but later she found out it was because she wasn't heading anywhere in particular, just walking around in circles.

She checked her map and groaned. She had taken a wrong turn while trying to get to Emerald Park, but she couldn't turn back and correct her mistake as she didn't know exactly where she was at that moment. Courtney was lost.

- Chapter 6 -

Guilty

There she was, standing in the middle of nowhere, with no signs leading her to a place she saw on her map and nobody she could ask for directions.

All the optimism and positivity she was feeling a while ago were slowly disappearing. She had no idea where she was, and nobody was there to help her. Courtney had never felt this desolate and disconnected from the rest of the world.

The more she walked, the more physically and mentally lost she felt. The only option was to sit down on the side of this deserted road and pray somebody would casually walk by and be able to help her.

She waited patiently. Every passing second felt like a whole minute, every minute like an hour. It didn't look like anybody was going to find her anytime soon, and it wouldn't do her any good to sit around. That way, she would never be found. She tightly shut her eyes, and her tensed body started to relax - she hadn't realised that she was holding her breath until she exhaled slowly from her mouth and immediately felt much, much better.

Trembling, she stood up and decided to keep walking on the road, although it was not as dangerous with the absence of vehicles. She tried to find a place she could recognise on her map.

Courtney checked her watch. It was already after dinnertime, and she wasn't back home - like she thought she may have been by now - brushing her teeth or reading in bed. No, instead she was walking in circles around a mysterious place with no idea how she ended up there in the first place. Yes, she was definitely having the time of her life but the guilt she felt in the pit of her stomach weighed her down slightly because she was leaving Amelia and Mum at home to worry about her, but she didn't stop.

She shook her head and talked herself into continuing her journey, but on the inside, she was itching to rest and have a quick bite to eat. If she continued walking and running or stayed up any longer without eating anything, she might become seriously ill - so she settled on finding her way out of there the following day.

Her only option now was to find a little patch of grass where she could rest for the night, but the eerie place only housed plants that were altitudinous trees that looked like they were tall enough to reach the clouds.

Surprisingly, cars were parked in driveways and the houses looked pretty new, but nobody was to be seen outside in this quiet village.

The closest thing to a little bit of grass that Courtney could reach was a tiny plastic houseplant perched on top of someone's car - but potted plants shouldn't be on cars!

That's when Courtney began to realise that everything about this unfamiliar setting seemed quite peculiar, like the fact that one of the pointed roofs of the aligned houses had a plastic lawn flamingo balancing on it, and if she craned her neck as far as it could go, she could see that something was growing on the trees - and that that something was a pair of shoes!

No, it couldn't be. Potted plants on top of cars? Lawn flamingos on pointed roofs? Shoes on trees?! This was probably a dream or a hallucination.

Courtney hadn't eaten in a long while - maybe she was dizzy. She sat down on the hard, roughly paved sidewalk and pulled a sandwich from her bag. She hadn't realised how hungry she was up until now - and she wished she could have a steaming bowl of her mother's signature vegetable soup and a tall glass of warm milk. Instead, she had a cold grilled cheese sandwich and a few sips of water for dinner. She dreaded the long, cold days ahead where she would have to sleep outside every night at midnight, wake up at the crack of dawn, and live off cold grilled cheese sandwiches, apple and carrot slices, and orange juice boxes. This was not the way she wanted to spend her school vacation.

Maybe she was exaggerating a little, but it still wasn't the best way to spend one's vacation, that's for sure. Courtney's stomach continued to make gurgling sounds even after she ate her sandwich, but the rest of the food she had packed was to be saved until she could find more. She looked around her once more.

The town still seemed odd; it couldn't have just been a figment of her imagination. She decided to try and find out how to get out of there first thing in the morning because now, it was bedtime. And that was how she fell asleep: confused, tired, and still hungry, on the rough sidewalk of an unknown destination.

- Chapter 7 -

Surprise, Surprise

"Ouch!" Courtney exclaimed, massaging her head softly.

Something had fallen from the sky and landed right on top of her, it then fell on the floor beside where she was sitting. She picked it up and carefully examined it to discover that the mysterious object that caused her head to throb was a worn-out, steel-toe brown boot that looked like it might have belonged to a giant at one point.

Courtney looked up at the sky and found the matching pair of the boot on one of the shoe trees. Judging from the colour of the sky and the blinding sun rays, Courtney could tell that it was time for her to get up and find a way out of... well, wherever she was right now.

She stood up and stretched, and her joints cracked like fireworks. She was still a little tired, but if she waited until she was fully ready to find a way out of the strange place then she might as well move in.

She adjusted her ponytail, slung her backpack over her shoulder, and headed forward; she didn't know why, but she just had a feeling that this was the direction she needed to move in so she could find the exit of this completely deserted town... or was it?

Just as she stood up, Courtney heard a scurrying sound that seemed to be coming from behind her. She swivelled her head backward, but she didn't see anything that might have been emitting the noise.

But that wasn't all. She decided she wasn't going to leave until she found the source of the mysterious sound, however silly that may be. She just couldn't have lived with the thought that she may have been followed at one point in her life and did not have any information about it whatsoever. This was a matter she was getting to the bottom of.

She looked around. Right, left- then right again. But it was quite peculiar...

there weren't many places a person or an animal could hide - no bushes or benches anything could duck behind.

So, again, Courtney concluded that it was all nothing but a figment of her imagination. But what she saw next was very real.

Katie Clover sat down on the kitchen table, slowly stirring the microwaveable mashed potatoes and lumpy gravy that was her dinner.

"Mumm... no offence, but I don't want to eat your microwave dinners anymore," she whined, "one more day and I'm going to puke."

Her mother sighed and plopped down on the seat next to her daughter, holding her own bowl of soggy mashed potatoes. "It's all we have, so eat it or starve," Mrs. Clover snapped. She shovelled a spoonful into her mouth, swallowed it, and replied, "But you're right; this is revolting."

Katie saw an opportunity ahead, and her eyes lit up. "Can dad order takeout, then?" But she had gotten her hopes up too high.

A firm 'No,' was all she got back.

"Eat. Quickly," Katie looked down at her now cold dinner, she decided to follow her mother's advice - and starve.

So, when Mrs. Clover had her back turned (trying

to figure out whether or not she could freeze milk and microwave it two weeks later to keep it from spoiling), Katie made a dash to the bin and emptied her entire bowl inside.

Mrs. Clover turned around. "Finished? Already?" she gasped in disbelief.

Katie quickly turned her chuckle into a cough so her mother would believe that her daughter finished her dinner in under a minute when she had just been complaining about how much she hated it.

"Yes, I'm finished," Katie grinned, "but don't ever make me eat that again. Just because I-um, gulped it all down in one minute, doesn't mean I liked it. I wish you would start cooking a bit more like Courtney's mum; while I'm sitting here trying to get the taste of cold, defrosted gravy out of my mouth, Courtney's probably having a delectable meal of fish and chips, courtesy of Mrs. Carter."

And that's when Katie saw Courtney jogging past her house. She rubbed her eyes and blinked, but when she opened her eyes, Courtney was still outside her door, inspecting a map of sorts. But it can't have been Courtney. Her mind was just playing tricks on her. How ironic would it be, to be talking about your best friend with your mother to then actually find her strolling past your front door?

Just to make sure, though, Katie told her mother about seeing (or rather, imagining) Courtney walking right past them. As soon as Mrs. Clover stood up to confirm Katie's words, Courtney was gone. What a bizarre day for Katie, first arguing about Courtney with her mum, actually seeing her, and then missing the opportunity to show her mother and prove she hadn't gone mad which Katie thought bitterly, could have been a big possibility when you come to think about it.

But what if Katie wasn't imagining? What if Courtney was indeed strolling around this neighbourhood? If so, why?

However strange that incident might have seemed to Katie, it wasn't the strangest thing she would learn about her best friend.

- Chapter 8 -

Not Alone

Courtney was feeling incredibly queasy, and not because of the cold sandwich she had eaten for breakfast. She was still looking for the creature lurking in - wherever it was hiding.

Five minutes. Ten minutes. Fifteen. Courtney was positive she heard something - and it was really bothering her that she couldn't see anything. She gave up on trying to find it, and set her priorities: look for a way to get out of here and to Emerald Park. Search for the door (if not in Emerald Park, then keep looking). Find out what the problem is beyond the gates and a way to solve it, to protect your loved ones.

She continued to walk, trying her best to forget

about the sound she heard. Until she heard a much more startling one.

"Hullo," said Katie Clover sheepishly.

She had been found. Courtney was speechless, but when she was able to talk, the first sound that came out of her mouth was an ear-splitting scream.

"Katie?" she stammered. "W-what are you doing here?" It wasn't every day she saw her best friend in an unknown place whilst on a run to save the world. Wow, events like that always sound more heroic than they actually are.

Katie raised her eyebrows questioningly at Courtney. "Well, that depends on where 'here' is." It was Courtney's turn to look at her friend questioningly now.

"And may I please know why you started following me, when, and what you're doing here, of all the places in this world?" Her expression was a cross between joy, to see her best friend, anger, at the fact that Katie was following her around without telling her, and relief at knowing she wasn't alone in this unsettling setting, but Katie's expression remained sheepish.

"It all started when my mother made another one of her gruesome microwave dinners," she started, "mum was insisting that I eat my entire bowl of mashed potatoes, (which tasted as though they were in the freezer longer than I was on this planet) and I had a different idea of a perfect meal. It ended up as an argument between us, and then your mum, well, she was kind of... sort of dragged into it."

"My mum?" said Courtney. "What does my mother have to do with the argument between you and your mum?"

Katie shook her head. "Don't worry, all I said was that her cooking was great." She reassured her friend. And she resumed with the telling of how she ended up following Courtney, sparing no details. She kept talking until she reached the point where Courtney was outside her window.

"And you followed me?" Courtney shook her head, half exasperated, half amused. Katie nodded. Secretly, Courtney was glad to see her friend. It meant she didn't have to be alone. Yes, she had to find the door on her own, and yes, the warning was meant for her - but what if she just took Katie along to stay by her side, without informing her much about what she was actually doing - she could just spare the details, couldn't she? Of course, it wasn't that easy with a friend as curious as Katie, but it was better than going alone. That could also be a way of helping herself - seeing others she loves around her.

"Katie," she peeped, "since you're already here, would you be able to accompany me, just until I get home?"

Katie looked at Courtney suspiciously. "What are you doing here though? I gave you the full story; the answers to all your questions and the reasons behind all your enquiries. Now it's your turn to spill your secret."

Courtney didn't know what to say. She was flabbergasted. But Katie had a right to know...

"I'll tell you later, I promise. Now, I have to get to Emerald Park as soon as possible."

And just like that, the girls were off to Emerald Park, Katie almost bursting with questions, but she could see that Courtney was incredibly tired by the big purple bags under her eyes, and she could be easily irritated in this state. She offered her friend a banana. "No, thanks, I don't like bananas," was what she got back. To be honest, she didn't like bananas either, but had only brought a bunch along because it was the only food her mum didn't stuff in the freezer... and she was pretty sure apples wouldn't exactly taste the same after coming out of the blast chiller.

The duo only paused to check the map every so often, but other than that, they kept their mission ahead of them. Well, maybe Katie not so much, but she was still determined to help her best friend out, despite not really knowing the real reasons for why she was following Courtney on the mysterious search or adventure she was on. And if it was Emerald Park she wanted to go to, Emerald Park is where she will be. They may not have talked much, but it was just the presence of her friend that put Courtney's mind at ease. They found themselves back at Katie's in no time and planned their route to the majestic garden of wonders from there.

"I know the way from here," Katie finally declared.

Courtney stuffed the map in her backpack as Katie steered them right, straight, left, then right again. Time flew by quickly, and suddenly the girls found themselves standing right in front of a marvellous statue made entirely out of pure emerald, of a peacock. That was their welcome into Emerald Park, and they both sighed with relief upon seeing the statue, as they knew they had arrived. The journey might not have been as tiring when in each other's company, but it was still a long one to make, and an accomplishment nonetheless.

Silence hung in the air for the first few minutes in the outdoor paradise. No matter how many times you've been to Emerald Park, you will still be in awe when you take a walk around. The girls marvelled at everything they saw; even the ground looked much cleaner and fancier than the one at Bliss Park.

"What exactly are we looking for here?" Katie asked. "Because I know you didn't run away from home without any supervision just to take a stroll around the park, although it is quite a spectacular park," she added thoughtfully, looking around and watching the birds fly across a clear blue sky dotted with the fluffiest white clouds you could imagine. It was hard to believe that the clouds were grey and the weather was damp and gloomy just a few days ago.

That's when Courtney decided to tell Katie everything... except a tiny voice at the back of her head was warning her not to get anyone involved in this dangerous escapade - who knows what would be waiting behind the door? It would be wrong to put anyone else through what she had to face. So she settled on skipping the details.

"I'm looking for a gate."

Katie raised an eyebrow. "A gate? All this distance we covered, and I don't even know where on earth you were before I followed you - all that was for a gate? You really are a crazy friend... I don't know whether I admire you for it, or whether I'm a little scared of you!" She laughed, but Courtney could tell she was slightly annoyed. Katie was awful at hiding her emotions.

Courtney pretended not to notice, although deep down, she felt incredibly guilty for dragging Katie into her mess. She didn't blame her for being upset. She also knew it was taking all of Katie's self-control not to blurt out all the questions she had in mind, and as her best friend, Courtney appreciated that completely.

Taking a deep breath, Courtney managed to plaster a half-smile on her face. "Yes, I'm looking for a gate... a really old and withered wooden one, with overgrown plants all over it."

Katie looked around and shrugged. "Doesn't look like a place where you could find many overgrown plants and withered wood around here," she told Courtney. "Just immaculately trimmed bushes and young evergreen trees with their barks shooting straight out of the perfect grass."

Courtney knew her friend was right. Just like in Violet Valley, Courtney could tell that the door she was hunting for was incredibly unlikely to be found where she was right now. So she was moving on. "Next park: Grow Garden. It's closest to where we are now." she looked at Katie and expected her to follow along, but Katie's phone just happened to chime. She had gotten a message from...

"Mum!" Katie gasped. "She's asking me where I am!"

Courtney felt even more guilty now. Why had she asked Katie to join her? She was already making her own mother miserable - why Mrs. Clover too?

She took this as her own responsibility, and she was the one who had to fix it. "Don't reply, for now, just go back home and tell her you were in the backyard all along. It works for me," she said with a shrug.

Katie nodded, thanked Courtney, and gave her the bunch of bananas she had brought along with her. "Just in case," she winked.

Courtney couldn't be more grateful for her best friend. Not necessarily for the bananas, but for the kind approach. She put them in her bag and continued walking.

- Chapter 9 -

The Final Destination

Courtney began her journey to Grow Garden. She had been there a couple of times already when she was younger. It was a small, friendly open area with designated spots for visitors to plant their own seeds; whether from home or the little booths they had in the garden. Overall, it was a nice place and an easy one for Courtney to look in.

She pulled out her map once more. The journey was a little longer than she had anticipated, but she didn't mind that much and took this as an opportunity to get some exercise.

If Courtney wasn't so enthusiastic about everything all the time, she would not have been able to complete her journey, her journey to find some answers to the cryptic dream that she had, that has since consumed her entire existence. Her optimism was a gift – and she was going to take full advantage of that. Instead of thinking 'The door isn't here', she would think 'That's one park closer to all the answers I need'.

It helped. This was not a never-ending search, to Courtney, it was an enthralling journey. And Courtney was going to enjoy as much of it as she could.

The hours passed like minutes as Courtney got closer to Grow Garden. She reached there quickly without realising and felt a rush of happiness as she realised what she had accomplished.

She remembered to set her watch timer before doing anything else and began examining the area, scanning for anything that might have looked out of place amongst all the ripe tomatoes and organic cucumbers, but the door she was searching for was too old - and too vast - for this garden.

It was time for Courtney to visit Willow Garden... the last destination. If the door was not there, then it wasn't within reach at all for Courtney. It all depended solely on the last park.

Willow Garden was just about forty-five minutes away on foot, and Courtney took that as good news. The farther she would have to go to look for Willow Garden, the longer she would need to walk to reach home, and compared to the rest of her journey, forty-five minutes was not that far.

The busy bees buzzed and the birds chirped cheerful songs whilst gliding across the sky like kites. Courtney was not only excited to find the door to this last destination, but she was trying to enjoy the pleasant scenery as much as possible - the environment she was in was absolutely beautiful and sent her spirits soaring higher than fireworks on New Year's Eve.

To fuel her energy, Courtney pulled out one of her last sandwiches, which she nibbled on slowly so they would last the whole way. She was surprised that her mother hadn't called her yet, but she took it as a good sign. It meant she wasn't worrying too much - which was great. Courtney's trip was slowly turning from tiring to empowering. She was definitely helping herself when she was being positive.

Although she wouldn't have to look any further than Willow Garden, that didn't mean it was an easy search. It was not an easy park to search, with all its twisted paths and overgrown grass... perfect for playing and rolling around in, but not exactly the best place to search for something. Especially something also covered in grass, plants, and moss.

Courtney began to realise that the gate was probably this park all along; it seemed very likely as she thought about it. It was not fear or dread causing her to tremble slightly as she took her first step in the park, but excitement. She could hardly contain it as she looked around and pushed through a colossal willow tree's drooping branches as if they were merely curtains she was pulling open. The willow tree was the symbol of this garden. Larger by far than any other tree in the area, it represents good luck and opportunities, and Courtney could feel the magic within its roots as she pushed deeper through its smooth leaves.

She emerged from the tree's shadows with her hair covered in leaves and small twigs, but she didn't care. However overgrown or disorganised this park may be, it still felt more magical to Courtney than any other park she had visited over the past couple of days. It was nature at its finest, and that beats elegance, immaculateness, and prestige. She had a strong feeling this was it, what she came to find.

Courtney didn't know exactly where she was going, but she let her feet guide her all the way. Even if you were to visit this park every single day, you would never know how to get everywhere without getting lost. But that was the beauty of it; you come across and learn a new path every time.

Courtney came across a fork later on while walking on her path. Without pausing to think, she took the path on the right and continued to walk. It was like the door was attracting her its way, guiding her to where she desired to be the most. She was surprised at how she knew, but she just did.

Courtney didn't pause to rest or to check the time, not even once, since she first arrived, because all she needed was to find the door, solve her problems and get back home. Home sweet home.

With every step she took, she moved a little faster, and without realising it, she was flying through the split paths confidently, swerving left and right.

She would occasionally find a person or a group of people who appeared to be lost, and they were all stunned by Courtney's effortlessness in navigating her path, and better yet, her ability to help them, even when she didn't know the pathways herself. But today, she was feeling lucky, and she could do anything.

After expelling such a great amount of energy, Courtney began to get a little tired, but her desire to find the door at last beat her desire to sit down and rest, so she carried on. But after a few more minutes of walking, her muscles began to ache, and she drew the line there.

She took a seat on a soft, vibrant patch of grass on the side of the path she was walking on, but couldn't contain her excitement and immediately got back up and running again, ignoring the slight pain in her knees.

Minutes passed, and then hours. Courtney didn't know how long she had been in Willow Garden, and she didn't care, either. All she wanted was to go through the gate and find out what was lurking behind it.

She wasn't scared; Courtney loved a good thrill, an exciting adventure, or an epic journey. And getting all that and a chance to protect the ones close to her heart was a dream come true for the thirteen-year-old.

Unknowingly, Courtney reached her last fork in the journey. She took a left, and walked on the straight path ahead of her for a few minutes, until...

- Chapter 10 -

The Unexpected

On the night of her competition, Amelia Carter was sprawled across her bed, a satisfied grin plastered on her face. A gleaming gold medal hung proudly up on the wall beside countless others. It glittered in the dim shade lamp Amelia kept by her bed every night.

All her science revision books lay open on her desk. She hadn't bothered to put them away when she returned home. She made it past the sorting, and she was ecstatic but that didn't mean she was done... Tomorrow, she would start revising for the finals. Her motto was 'You can never be too prepared'.

It was one of her easiest competitions, only second to maybe the one where all her contestants were homesick, and she just took the gold medal without having to do anything. But Amelia didn't like that; she liked to earn her medals and to deserve them, she needed to work hard and put in her maximum effort. And today was no exception.

Courtney was not there to support Amelia, and it felt a little unusual. But once she turned her full attention to the questions in front of her, and did her best to be the first to answer them, her quiz competitions didn't feel so different.

Amelia yawned. It was 2:00 am, and she had to sleep, but Amelia always wrote in her journal after every competition, to keep track of her progress. Ten minutes would be enough to sum up everything that happened in the competition. She would write about the types of questions she got, her opponent's skills, and things she could improve in the next competition. The list after this competition and the last one seemed to be noticeably shorter, and Amelia beamed with pride at the fact that she was improving.

Amelia wanted to surprise Courtney with her good news the next day, and couldn't wait to see the expression of happiness and delight on her younger sister's face. Thinking about Courtney put Amelia's mind at ease... but she wasn't going to be seeing Courtney anytime soon.

Amelia's mother already knew that her youngest daughter wouldn't be coming back the day she promised, but she didn't want Amelia to know that just yet. And that was exactly what Amelia dreamt about that night - good news she falsely hoped to deliver and a reunion she wouldn't get to make the following day.

The next morning, Amelia woke up with last night's grin still stuck on her face. The only thing that was even better than winning was being treated normally again. Her mother had no reason to treat her any differently today.

She went down for breakfast, and sure enough,

her mother wasn't down there, cooking up a storm. Amelia took the milk carton from the fridge and poured herself a bowl of cereal. Today, everything would be back to normal. Courtney would be back, her mother wouldn't find the need to treat her any differently - Amelia's exact definition of 'normal'.

She grabbed her favourite book from the vast bookshelf in the living room and curled up on the reclining armchair with her breakfast in her lap. Amelia was in her happy place - book in hand, breakfast, comfortable armchair... it was a whole new world in which she could forget all her real issues. In which she could learn to empathise with other people, expand her imagination and glide through the realms of literature. All she had to do was open a book.

Mrs. Carter once worked as a librarian, and she was the one who introduced her daughters to the beautifully artistic world that was reading.

Ever since they were little, the sisters would always

have their noses buried in a novel or an encyclopaedia. Courtney and Amelia were still bookworms, but Amelia since found that her favourite genre was non-fiction, whilst Courtney had always been obsessed with fantasy.

Occasionally, Courtney would borrow a science book from Amelia, and Amelia would ask for a fantasy novel from Courtney. All the books were fine. In fact, despite Amelia's love for reading non-fiction, her favourite book of all time was a classic play by Shakespeare: 'Romeo and Juliet'. That was the book open on her lap as she drank the last drops of milk straight from her cereal bowl; a habit she and her sister had that drove their mother up the wall.

Amelia missed fooling around with Courtney, and she wished she could revisit the days when the two of them were always being silly together. But she was fifteen, and that was no longer an option.

She placed her empty cereal bowl on the table

beside her. Another thing she did that her mother didn't like was eat in the living room. And another was reading in the kitchen. So basically, anything that involved food and a book was frowned upon by her mother. But maybe that was just because Mrs. Carter was a librarian - she always felt like she had to apply the same rules at home that she did in the library: no eating around a book, returning every single book exactly where she found it, being completely silent whenever someone's reading, and much, much more.

It was about time her mother turned their flat into a library. Amelia shuddered at the thought of bookshelves everywhere around the house. She liked books, but she also needed her own space. She directed her thoughts back to the book in her hands.

Amelia read for hours without realising. She had settled down for book breakfast and, before she knew it, her mother called her for her book club meeting.

"Already?! But it's too early for that!" she wondered whether her mother just mixed up the times or if she lost control of time whilst reading - again.

She checked her watch, and without saying a word, got ready for her meeting and was off. Usually, Courtney would come with her and participate in the meetings being held in the neighbourhood, but this time it was just Amelia.

Next week, Courtney would join her again.

Or would she?

- Chapter 11 -

A Whole New World

There it was, old and antiquated, but magical in every way. This was the moment Courtney was waiting for... the door was in front of her very eyes.

Her pulse quickened and her hand trembled slightly as she reached out to push the gates open.

As soon as her fingertips touched the withered wood, Courtney felt an electric surge throughout her entire body. With a strong push, the door creaked open and Courtney stepped inside, careful to leave the door open behind her.

She didn't know what to expect, but it definitely wasn't what she was seeing right before her.

Sweeping rivers and waterfalls seemed to shimmer and sparkle around her, and exquisite creatures fluttered and glided in the air.

The mysterious place was full of life. Yet, she was the only one present. But she would soon discover, that would be temporary.

"Hello, there!"

Courtney was deeply surprised to hear a voice beside the ones in her head. It was very light and airy, like a whisper, but Courtney was absolutely sure she heard something. She slowly wheeled around, and saw a beautiful young lady, about the same age as her mother, standing behind her.

The lady had long, thick eyelashes, and pale skin, and wore a lot of jewellery. She wore a long purple gown that billowed around her, even though there was no breeze to assist. She smiled warmly at Courtney, and, even though she didn't know the woman, Courtney immediately warmed to her.

"My name is Violet, can I help you?" she spoke once more, with that same gentle whisper. Courtney felt like she could trust the lady. She told her everything, from the beginning until the end, and when she was done, Violet's eyes lit up and grew twice their normal size. Her warm smile disappeared.

"Follow me," she said but her voice had lost its welcoming airy tone, and it was replaced with a cold, commanding one. Courtney wondered what she said to upset Violet, but she was too afraid to ask. So she just followed along, silent as a mouse.

Every once in a while, as they walked the scenery around them would change from grassy meadows, to enchanted forests, to crystal mountains, each view was as magical as the other.

A few minutes later, Violet spoke once more, and her airy whisper returned, as did her warm smile.

"Forgive me for being quite harsh, my dear. It was just that - they have been waiting for your arrival for a very long time. And here you are now!" Violet was beaming at Courtney. "But I never got your name." Her face constant with her beaming and unwavering smile.

"It's Courtney," Courtney replied. "Courtney Carter, and I'm flattered, but... I think you have the wrong person. All I wanted to do was help my friends and family," but she couldn't help adding, "who are 'they', though? Who has been waiting for me?"

"You'll see," Violet said with a wink. She took Courtney's hand into her own and led her to wherever they were going.

Courtney didn't ask Violet where she was taking her but decided to look around instead to take in the wondrous surroundings. Then her stomach began to gurgle and grumble.

"Hungry?" Violet asked.

Courtney nodded. Violet rummaged in her bag

for a while, then pulled out a sandwich for Courtney.

"Thank you so much!" Courtney couldn't have been more grateful. Violet grinned but said nothing.

They walked for nearly an hour but to Courtney, it felt much shorter. Because she had company. She noticed something glittering in the distance but it wasn't glittering like a gel pen or a glittery notebook - it glimmered like the light of a thousand stars combined, so bright that it could be seen from many miles away.

Courtney noticed that they were heading toward the light. It became bigger and bigger the closer they got. Soon, they were close enough for Courtney to distinguish the glittery shape, and suddenly, she was awestruck.

- Chapter 12 -

Inside a Fantasy

Right before Courtney's very eyes stood a magnificent and twinkling castle, with spiralling towers and silver flags. Encompassing it, were unique flowers and creatures that seemed to have the same dazzling glow as the castle. But upon closer view, Courtney discovered that the 'creatures' were actually...

"Fairies!" She looked up at Violet and smiled. "Where are we?"

"We're here," she whispered softly and led Courtney to the gates of the castle.

"Wait!" Courtney yelled abruptly, just as they were about to enter. "I can't enter a place like this wearing my sneakers and sweaty gym clothes!"

Violet laughed. "You won't need to worry about that," she assured Courtney, "after you."

As soon as her foot touched the pearly floor of the grand hall, Courtney's sneakers turned into silver slippers, her gym attire into a lilac gown, and her messy, tangled strawberry-blonde hair into a magnificent bun, ornamented with fragrant flowers.

"Good evening, Violet," a guard inside the castle greeted Violet as soon as she stepped through the charming and magical doorway.

"Good evening, Sir William," she replied with a polite nod in his direction. "I wish to see the Empress."

"I'm afraid the Empress is busy this evening. I genuinely apologise for any inconvenience," Sir William told Violet. But she wasn't discouraged.

"I have the next Carter."

Those five words shocked the guard, and he trembled from head to toe. "I- I'll arrange for the two of you to see her this evening," he stuttered. Then he bowed and led them inside the Grand Hall.

Violet smiled at Courtney. "Welcome to Pearl Palace, home of the fairies and our Empress Tulip," she said with one of her signature smiles.

Courtney was speechless. Less than a minute ago, she was wearing her old t-shirt and leggings, half of her hair hanging out of her messy ponytail. Now she was in a spectacular palace, looking like a true princess. But something didn't feel right.

"It's amazing to be here," she told Violet, "but I only came to help my family and friends. I don't deserve any of this."

Violet gave her a reassuring smile. "Don't worry, you will have the opportunity to tell the Empress about that later this evening. But until then, why don't you just relax and enjoy yourself? Come on,

I'll introduce you to some people," she said, leading Courtney around the once spacious hall that was now packed with fluttering guests.

She took Courtney to the centre of the hall, where a petite young fairy was hovering and mingling with a group of fairies. "Courtney, meet Lily. Lily, this is Courtney Carter."

Lily's jaw dropped. She shook Courtney's hand, then looked at Violet. "Is she really the next Carter?" she asked. Violet nodded. "At least I think so. That's why I requested a meeting with the Empress."

Lily began to ask Courtney numerous questions - most of which she didn't know the answer to - and soon enough, all her friends joined in. Violet could tell her younger companion was feeling pressured, so she called her over to the other side of the room.

Courtney met many new people. Most of them she enjoyed being introduced to, and all of them stared and whispered when they heard her name.

She heard things like 'Heiress of Magic', 'the selected one' and of course, 'The next Carter'.

Time flew by like sand in an hourglass. As Violet was introducing Courtney to Holly, Daniel, and Joy, Sir William walked up to them and announced that they could now see the Empress.

"Excellent," Violet said, then clapped her hands once. Well, it was great seeing you once more, and I'm sure Courtney was glad to meet you, but we really should get going. Come on, Courtney." Violet shook the fairies' hands and followed Sir William with Courtney following behind them towards the stairs. Although at first, Courtney didn't recognise them as stairs, more as drifting clouds that sparkled and elevated up into the room above. It turns out the 'stairs' were more solid than they looked.

Led by Sir William, the trio proceeded up the shimmering staircase and walked down a narrow hallway, before stopping in front of a door so bright it looked like it was made of pure gold. Sir

William stepped back, and Violet knocked gently. The door remained shut.

A few minutes later, Violet attempted to knock again but again, found no luck in getting someone to open the door.

As they grew more and more impatient, Sir William gently pushed the door open and then stepped aside so that Violet and Courtney could enter. But as soon as they stepped foot in the room, Courtney immediately sensed that something was wrong...

Behind a desk of rose quartz was a tall-backed desk chair, completely empty except for a little piece of paper with hasty writing scribbled on it using red ink.

Violet picked up the note, and her face was as pale as the moon once she finished reading it. Lines of worry were etched on her face, and her hands trembled. She passed the note to Sir William, who abruptly wore the same reaction.

"What does it say?" Courtney asked, overthinking the endless possibilities of the piece of paper and the absence of the Empress. Was it a ransom note? A note of resignation, perhaps? Or was it something else? Although she didn't read the note herself, Courtney was already starting to feel sick.

Violet mustered up a weak smile, although her eyes were still wide with fear. "It's nothing for you to worry about dear... but we won't be seeing Empress Tulip today, I'm afraid. Your concerns and enquiries will have to wait until further notice."

Courtney still wanted to know what it was that made Violet lose her airy cheerfulness so abruptly, but she didn't push. This had happened before, when Courtney told Violet about her strange dreams. Did it perhaps have something to do with that?

"You will have the chance to see the Empress at some point, but until then, you can stay here at the palace. I will depart now, but I will only be gone temporarily. Sir William, please tell the rest of the guards to maximise security. I will inform the other fairies." And with a swish of her violet cloak, Violet was gone.

"I'll show you around the palace in a moment. If you could just stay here while I quickly call the guards, that would be splendid," Sir William bowed to her then rushed past her and out of the golden door.

Courtney was frightened... What was going on? But the reality of the situation was far worse than her predictions, and she felt helpless standing in the missing Empress's office.

- Chapter 13 -

Alone

The Grand Hall was buzzing with noise. Fairies of all sizes and colours were either whispering to one another, eyes wide as saucers or fleeing Pearl Palace before another tragedy could occur.

A fairy was standing beside the door of Empress Tulip's office when Sir William opened the door, and after peeking inside, she discovered that the Empress was no longer present behind her crystal quartz desk.

Then she told another fairy, and the news spread like wildfire across the room, but some people exaggerated what they heard, and twisted tales were formed. Violet came storming down the stairs and magically magnified her voice so it could be heard by everyone in the room over all the noise.

"Everyone, please listen. I know most of you have heard about the Empress not being present in Pearl Palace at the moment, although some of you may have the wrong idea of what happened. I am simply going to ask you not to worry as the Empress will return shortly," she announced and swiftly walked out of the crystal castle gates.

Courtney stood in Empress Tulip's office for what seemed like forever, not knowing exactly what she was waiting for, albeit she knew one thing: she was not in the best possible position.

Violet departed, the Empress was nowhere to be found, and she was standing alone in the monarch's empty office.

After waiting for what seemed like hours, Sir William came back into the Empress's office to show Courtney around the palace she was staying in.

There were many doors, all identical to the gate she hunted for before arriving at Pearl Palace, except newer and freshly painted. Despite the enormous number of rooms and hallways in the palace, Sir William only showed her three; the Grand Hall, the dining room, and her private chambers, where he left her offering a final curtsy.

Courtney lay on her bed and looked at the ceiling. Her room looked simple yet stunning: it wasn't very large but it was more than enough space for the thirteen-year-old. A miniature chandelier hung from the ceiling, illuminating the bare, spotless walls. Her bed - an elegant four-poster, draped with powder blue curtains - was tucked in the corner of the room, with a pink quartz nightstand made out of the same material as the Empress's desk beside it. Her wardrobe was small and simple, with two dresses hung inside: an elegant gown, for special occasions, and a casual dress for everyday use. Courtney sat on the corner of her bed and sighed.

She was in an enchanted castle, surrounded by fairies and magic, yet she desperately missed her life back home. She missed her mother and her sister. She missed her best friend. And, of course, she missed her books.

Just when Courtney changed out of her ball gown and into the comfortable dress that was left in her closet, a white light lit up in her room, signalling the start of dinner. She exited her room and ambled down the floating stairs and into the dining hall, where around half of the remaining fairies were seated around a vast dining table piled high with an aromatic array of food and pastries, enough to keep an entire city well-fed for a week. At the very end of the table was a vacant quartz throne, decorated with light green gemstones and velvet cushioning. Courtney couldn't take her eyes off the throne; the sheer beauty of it was alluring on its own - Courtney couldn't imagine how welcoming it would be to see the Empress of a fairy dwelling seated upon it.

Dinner at Pearl Palace was usually a pleasant experience with open conversations, but that day, Courtney only witnessed group murmuring and paired whispering, the eyes of the fairies constantly darting towards the empty throne. She felt quite uncomfortable and isolated, seated on her own near the corner of the table with no one to talk to or express her emotions to. She wished Violet was around to comfort her and remind her that everything would be alright. She desperately needed that reminder.

- Chapter 14 -

Cover of Night

Violet sighed with relief and grinned. It was finally dusk outside Pearl Palace, and everything was going exactly as intended. Courtney had arrived at the palace, and she saw that the Empress wasn't there. She was an impulsive girl; she was bound to go looking for her any time now. And it was Violet's job to make sure Courtney wasn't going to find the empress anytime soon...

She smirked and strode away from the castle's double doors, her violet cloak billowing in the breeze behind her. It wouldn't be long before Courtney felt determined to find the Empress, and if she did now, it would ruin the entire scheme Violet had worked on for so long. So under the dark cover of night, she journeyed an incredible distance to the undisclosed location where Empress Tulip could be found, concealed from all eyes.

***

Amelia carried her breakfast on a tray and plopped down onto her favourite reclining armchair. She felt apprehensive and uneasy, and that feeling wasn't due to the fact that her competition finals were just one month away - her sister wasn't home. She was expecting her back home the evening after the sorting, but Courtney was nowhere to be found.

She sighed and took a sip of her orange juice. But the more she pondered the matter, the less it started to make sense: Courtney would never decide to make plans on the day of her competition, and she wasn't the type of person who would just go missing after merely meeting with friends. Something was awry, and she was going to get to the bottom of it.

Amelia pushed her breakfast away. The sudden thought and mere possibility of Courtney being in trouble made her lose her appetite. Her little sister may have been a little irritating at times, but Amelia still loved her and found the need to ensure that Courtney was alright. She used the little information she knew to figure out what she didn't, and she was still left with little knowledge of where Courtney might have been.

She would start by asking her mother to contact Mrs. Clover, just to make sure Courtney definitely wasn't at Katie's, and if not, (which was very likely,) Amelia would have to ask people in her neighbourhood if they had seen her recently. And then it would be Amelia's job to look for her younger sister and ensure she was alright.

But it might be too late for all that. Anything could happen to Courtney at any moment, and she could be anywhere. Amelia would have to act herself - now.

She pulled her hair up into a ponytail, slipped into her knee-length boots, and swung her backpack over her shoulder. She left a note for her mother explaining where she was going and that she would be back... hopefully. But it was too late to rethink what she was doing at this point. The front door slammed shut with a crash, and just like that, Amelia was gone.

Little did she know that it would take a miracle for her to find her younger sibling.

- Chapter 15 -

Looking Up

Courtney finished eating dinner quickly and ran up to her room, where she decided to sleep early and get the day over with. She had no idea how close she was to completing the task which was the main reason she was here in the first place, but she did know that the situation she was in at the moment wasn't helping her much.

She regretted acting before thinking. She did end up finding the door, but she also ended up in this sticky situation... and the only way to get out of this one? More acting on instinct. It wasn't what any other person would do in this situation, but after all, Courtney wasn't 'any other person'. Courtney wasn't the type of girl who would go this far and then quit. She writes her own story, and if she's living in a chapter she doesn't like, then she isn't going to give up writing. She would make sure the story moves on, ensuring that it would get better and better... with her own twist. And right now, she desperately needed to turn the page, a new chapter, new opportunities. She was going to find the Empress and ask her for help. She was going to save her family. Things were finally looking up! The problem for Courtney is, she didn't know what she was actually saving her family from. At first, she didn't know if any of her dreams had any truth to them, but now after indeed finding the magical door and seeing the Pearl Palace, surely it all had to be true... unless all of this was a dream? Surely not!

But would the story end there? After all, what she achieved was almost impossible, and the targets she set herself were almost unreachable. Yet, she was able to do all that, and more. Then what? After she helps her loved ones, she couldn't live her normal life knowing that there were completely abnormal and intriguing creatures out there, each with their own unique story to tell. But she decided to deal with that when she had to and turned all her concentration to the matter of finding Empress Tulip.

Violet said she was going to settle everything, and that Courtney had no reason to worry, but she knew from personal experience that nobody could have everything under control, and everyone needs a little help every now and then. And if Violet helped her in the past, then Courtney would have to return that favour. But until then... she had to rest.

The next day, Courtney studied the shifts of the guards at the door, but it turns out there weren't any - It was just Sir William, who stood by the gates from 12 pm until midnight. Tomorrow, it was showtime.

At exactly 1 am, Courtney grabbed her backpack and changed into the clothes she had kept inside just in case. Then she quietly snuck out of her bedroom, climbed down the floating stairs (slowly, as she still wasn't used to them), and made it past the front gates.

Once again, Courtney felt like she had made a stupid decision. She was out in the streets within a different dimension, planning to locate and possibly save the life of a fairy monarch who also happened to be the only person who could help her save her family. The idea of running away from home to search for a gate that's centuries old in all the public parks and gardens of the city seemed sensible compared to this: she didn't know a single place here; there was no way that anyone could ever find the incredibly well-hidden empress here, especially if they were new to the place.

But, after all, Courtney wasn't 'anyone' so she wasn't discouraged by the realisation that she did something crazy: in fact, she took the setback as a challenge. After all, every good, heroic story has to have at least one crazy lunatic. She snickered and took out a blank piece of paper and a pen, and sketched out a rough map using the Palace as her compass and the wooden direction signs as her source.

Within a few minutes, she had an unfinished sketch of her location on the paper before her. You and I would have found that scarcely enough to navigate around a new dimension, but not Courtney. Of course not. She held the map inches away from her nose and walked around to what she thought was the rabbit hole hill, but then she put the map down to examine her surroundings only to find out that she had been walking in circles the whole time. It was expected of Courtney to do something this foolish, but it still irked her that she was getting nowhere. Right now, as she was fooling around, the Empress could be anywhere and in any situation.

And most of the time, the adults in her life were not the ones who got to the bottom of these issues; it was Courtney herself. Although it would be silly to compare this situation to the time Mr. Scrooge left the school for weeks at a time with the same excuse, "I had the flu". But Courtney knew that the flu doesn't last for weeks, and after a bit of investigation, she concluded that the teacher was spending his afternoons sprawled on the couch, watching television.

Right now, her case was much bigger than a lazy teacher's. People's lives were at stake. This was a serious issue, and it required a serious attitude.

- Chapter 16 -

Somewhere Calm

Violet was seated on a high-backed armchair beside a fireplace with flickering purple flames. Outside the window, dazzling specks of snow were drifting gracefully. In one hand, she held a steaming mug of hot cocoa with marshmallows and whipped cream, and with the other, she casually flipped the pages of a dusty spell book that was passed down generations in her family.

As she flipped the fragile yellowing parchment on which the most powerful spells known were written, she heard a knock on the door. But it wasn't a gentle, polite knock; whoever was outside must have been pretty desperate for Violet to open the door, because they were rapping on the door frantically.

After two minutes of continuous knocking, Violet could ignore the mysterious visitor no longer.

She placed the mug on a coaster and hid the book in her cupboard before opening the door, and once she did, she didn't let the visitor - a cold, shivering, cloaked old man - in because what he didn't know was that in the same room she was in right now, was a little bed covered in lacy blankets, and lying still upon it was the Empress of Pearl Palace, fast asleep.

"Can I help you?" Violet asked kindly, although her face said otherwise. She was pretty surprised to find a living soul besides herself and the Empress in this isolated place. But, of course, the old man couldn't find out that there was another person in the room, so she only kept the door open with a crack, her head poking out to talk to him.

He said nothing, so Violet asked again. "Can I help you?"

Once more, the old man, shivering on her doorstep,

said nothing - he just stood there, still as a statue. Violet felt like this man was trying to waste her time, so she tried to close the door. But just as she was about to slam it shut in his face, the man stuck his foot out in front of the door to prevent it from closing.

Impatient, Violet opened the door completely to tell the man to depart, and she forgot the consequences of showing the man what was behind that large piece of weathered wood. It seemed, however, that it was the exact opportunity the old man was waiting for because after taking a good glimpse of what was behind the door, he left without uttering a single word.

Furious, Violet began pacing back and forth, unsure of what to do. Just a few minutes ago, she was settled comfortably beside the fireplace with a steaming mug of cocoa, and now, she was in the worst state possible. Her biggest secret was exposed. She had no idea who that man was, how he got there, or why he wanted to see the Empress, but now that he had uncovered her secret, he could do anything with it. And if the wrong person found out, things would go downhill for Violet and Empress Tulip. But for Violet, they already were.

However upsetting the current situation was for Violet, she knew that it would do her no good to pace around her cottage. So, instead, she grabbed her coat, checked to make sure the Empress still was under her temporary sleeping enchantment, and left the cabin, shutting the door firmly behind her. She was going to fix this problem before it escalated into a catastrophe. Although, with someone like Courtney looking for the Empress, that was easier said than done...

Amelia was standing on the sidewalk of a busy road, panting and clutching a stitch in her side. She had just outrun a group of angry tourists because she had 'borrowed' one of their tour bikes, and when they found out the front wheel had already popped off. So she ditched her vehicle and ran quite a long distance on foot to shake them off her tail.

She was looking for Courtney, and she started off this journey with a fiery determination to bring her back. However, after just a few hours, she did feel the difficulty of the job she forced herself to do, and negative thoughts began to fill her brain, telling her that she would never be able to find her sister and that her absence would haunt her forever. However, she pushed them aside and continued by reminding herself that nothing would haunt her more than the fact that her sister was missing and that she did nothing about it. Even trying to find her was a good effort in itself, but Amelia wasn't satisfied with that. She would have to find her sister and bring her back home before feeling content, even if that meant spending weeks looking for her.

She knew it wouldn't be easy, and it didn't help

that she had no information whatsoever on where her sister could possibly be. A sigh escaped Amelia's lips. If she succeeded in this, Courtney would owe her for the rest of her life. But was she helping anyone by looking for Courtney, or was she just wasting her time, energy, and patience?

- Chapter 17 -

A Little Help

"Focus, Courtney. Focus, and you can do this. Focus, and you can help your loved ones. Focus, and you'll be a hero. And if not... then there will be consequences." Courtney had been hearing the same voice in her head, over and over again. It was the same voice that she heard in her dream (which she felt seemed like ages ago). But after hearing the same voice repeat the same words over and over in her head, she also realised that it sounded a lot like Violet, which resulted in the conclusion that Courtney was doing the right thing and that she was in the right place.

But was this new message motivation or a warning? And what could be the 'consequences' mentioned? At first, Courtney listened to the strange voice in her head and took it as a source of inspiration to carry on, but the more she thought about it, the more she thought about the consequences of her actions and not the positive side. That led to even more negative thoughts, and she even considered quitting once or twice. But deep inside, she knew that she could do this and that many people depended on her, and this fire in her heart kept her going when she felt the most discouraged. One day, she got exactly what she needed, for she overheard an old man wearing a rugged cloak talking to a young man with a bushy beard, and she caught the words 'Violet' and 'Pearl Palace', but what shocked her the most was when the old man said, 'Empress Tulip has gone missing. Have you not heard?'

She was in a different part of the new dimension, and she was surprised that the old man knew about the empress. However, she knew from a few experiences at school that news like this travels fast. So she moved in closer to hear the rest of the conversation between the two men, but just at that moment, the bearded man walked away, giving Courtney the chance to go up to the old man and ask him what he knew about the Empress and Pearl Palace.

"Hello, Sir," she said with a polite smile, "I overheard you talking to that man about Empress Tulip and Violet. I was wondering if you could tell me a little more about that matter, as that would help me greatly."

The man gave her a crooked, toothless grin and nodded. Then he pulled out a shaky hand, and Courtney dumped all the coins she had in her purse into his palm. As soon as he stuffed the money in a pocket on the inside of his cloak, he began to talk. "The Empress of Pearl Palace is currently being kept in an undisclosed location, far from this place. Only one living soul besides me and the Empress herself knows where that is, and that would be Violet," he divulged.

"But where is that undisclosed location?" Courtney enquired, hoping he wouldn't charge her any more for that essential piece of information, however, she was too hopeful, for he held out his hand once more. "I gave you all I have."

The old man grunted, his grin disappeared, and he raised an eyebrow questioningly at Courtney. "And why, if I may ask, do you want to know all this?" He asked her, curious as to why a dazed-looking thirteen-year-old would want to know the undisclosed location of the Empress. He didn't understand why young people always felt the need to know everything that didn't concern them. And Courtney told him her story, but she didn't get to finish it. Halfway through, he threw his arms into the air - as if she were reading the dictionary from beginning to end instead of telling him a thrilling tale about her epic journey - and yelled, "Alright, alright! Gosh, you have to bore me with the pathetic little story of how you got here! Empress Tulip is currently in a cottage located deep into the northern mountains of

Astria, which are very difficult to reach. Any hopes you have of saving her are empty, because even with all the powerful relations she has as the Queen of Astria and the Empress of Pearl Palace, nobody but me was able to find her, and even I couldn't save her."

Courtney was not discouraged in the slightest by the old man's words. And she figured that if those words didn't discourage her, then the message she kept hearing in her head shouldn't, either. And now, she had an incredibly useful piece of information she would definitely need in the journey ahead.

She just had one question...

"What's Astria?"

The old man looked at Courtney like she was completely bonkers, but Courtney's expression remained politely puzzled. He sighed, scratched his bald head, and said, "It's the entire dimension we're in right now - where have you been? Oh, right, that's- that's my bad, I forgot you weren't from around here," He hobbled off, leaving Courtney standing there grinning from ear to ear.

She pulled out her roughly sketched map, scribbled map of Astria across the top, and scanned it for any signs that could help her find her way into the northern mountains of Astria, but none were there. Courtney would have to wander around and hope her feet would lead her to the mountains.

- Chapter 18 -

Understood

After her encounter with the old man, Courtney broke down her journey into parts. First of all, she figured that the northern mountains of Astria must be up on the north side of Astria (and it didn't take her long to figure that one out). So that was where she was heading. The town directly to the north of the one she was currently in was Aurora Village, so that was where she was headed next.

While she was walking straight ahead, she wondered why the old man said it was incredibly difficult to get to the northern mountains. Was it the cold?

Were the mountains steep or uneven? Courtney

was sure she could handle that if she tried hard enough, and if all the fairies in Pearl Palace teamed up, that would be more than enough to locate the northern mountains of Astria, wouldn't it?

She knew it would be harder than that, and she wondered what difficulties she would face when she found the mountains... and even before that.

It helped a little when she found a discarded map of Astria - a proper map of Astria - on the floor in Aurora village. She knew without looking at it that the Northern mountains of Astria wouldn't be there, and she was correct. But the map could still help her find the mountains, indirectly.

She travelled for hours and hours, and only rested for minutes in between. She tried to get something to eat, but nobody would give her any food without receiving money in return. She opened her bag and rummaged inside for any leftover snacks, but all she found was the bunch of bananas that Katie had given her. She sighed as she slowly peeled one of them and took a large bite out of it. This was not the time to be picky.

She journeyed for days, and those days quickly became weeks. Courtney ate wild berries and fruits (she had collected plenty of those from Exotica, and kept the stash in her backpack), but whenever she got lucky, she would find a snack on the side of the pathways. She wondered why anyone would leave their food on the pathway, but she was grateful nonetheless.

She wondered about her mother and her sister. She hoped that Amelia had proceeded to the final of her competition and that her mother was doing well. She wished she could somehow reassure her mother that she was doing just fine, or get some company without being a burden to whoever joined her on this lonely journey. And one night, while she was wandering around the eastern border of Lightley, one of her wishes came true.

Arthur was a charming young lad born and raised in Lightley, Astria. He was brought up by his grandmother as his parents passed away in a tragic accident involving dark magic when he was just six years old. Now, at fifteen years old, he still lives with his grandmother and two brothers, aged seventeen and nineteen, in a cabin to the east of Lightley.

Growing up, the three brothers were very competitive, and Arthur was constantly being outshone by his older brothers. His grandmother constantly reminded him that he was dearest to her, but that still didn't seem to be enough compared to all the love and admiration his brothers received from the rest of Lightley.

His favourite thing to do was to take long strolls around the forest of Astria, located right after the eastern border of Lightley. Everyone all around Astria fears that forest, for many years ago, myths were going around that unpredictable perils and fatal creatures were lurking in the shadows of the intimidating redwood trees, thus making any hunters or human beings avoid it, if they can help it.

But not Arthur. He felt like he really connected with the forest and all its features. The sound of chirping birds and flowing waterfalls and the calming sight of the beads of sunlight seeping through the trees always put his mind at ease. But what Arthur found the most comforting about the forest was the lack of people. It was the perfect place to go in case he ever needed to be alone. That was, until Courtney showed up.

"Hi! Sorry to disturb you. I haven't seen another human in days! This place is full of animals, though. And rivers, and waterfalls. It's nice, despite the fact that it has a looming sense of danger about it. I don't know why, I just feel it. Can you tell me the way out of here, pleaaase?" She was talking a mile a minute, and she didn't stop to take a breath.

"Whoah, calm down! If you want me to actually understand you and help you, then start over, slowly! Or, if not, then I don't mind listening to you talk quickly all day," Arthur laughed.

Courtney blushed and giggled. "No, sorry, I just... I haven't seen a human being in a few days, so I just got a little excited."

She was blushing so furiously that her entire face resembled a tomato.

"How did you end up here?" Arthur asked, oblivious to her deep embarrassment. "I thought I was the only one crazy enough to wander around this place."

And Courtney told him everything, sparing no details and cutting off no parts. And Arthur listened, from the very start to the end. While she was talking, she couldn't help but notice the piercing blue shade of his eyes, and the long wavy hair that kept getting into them.

When she finished telling him her story, Arthur was so intrigued by her bravery, intelligence, and charm. He found that they had lots in common: they were both introverts and kept mostly to themselves, and both of them shared a love for fantasy books.

"So... have you heard of the Northern mountains of Astria?" Courtney asked matter-of-factly, already expecting the answer - but there was still an inkling of hope in her eyes.

Arthur shook his head, sympathetic to Courtney's difficult task. "I'm sorry, I haven't... but I can help you find it, and accompany you on your way to finding it. My jokes may be terrible, but I am good at providing company and optimism." He laughed.

Courtney chuckled. "You were the first person who willingly offered to help me throughout my entire trip, and I'm so grateful... but I don't want to be a burden or make anyone work for me - this is my responsibility, and I think I was supposed to fulfil it.

"But I won't be fulfilling it for you. I'll only be

helping you do it yourself. You've already accomplished so much - allow me to join you in your next steps. And you're not a burden at all! In fact, I'll be ecstatic at the chance to leave this place, it gets boring after a while," he said, making it nearly impossible for Courtney to say no, but they settled on completing the journey the next day as it was getting late and Courtney was worn out from all the walking she'd done.

Courtney began to realise that the more time she spent with Arthur, the more time she wanted to spend with him in the future.

- Chapter 19 -

Off The Hook

Violet was striding around a chained chair; she was glad this moment had come at last. Her blue coat and black high-heeled boots lay strewn across the floor. On the chair, gagged and tied, was the only person (besides Violet and Empress Tulip) who had ever set foot in the Northern Mountains of Astria.

It was the old man.

Violet yanked the cloth from his mouth. "Who did you tell?"

Her voice was harsh and commanding, and it sent shivers down the man's spine.

"Nobody."

He tried his best to sound confident with his answer, but his voice quavered nervously, and Violet could tell that wasn't his honest answer.

"Liar!" she snarled. "Tell me. TELL ME! Who did you tell? Who knows the location of the Empress?"

The old man could take the pressure no longer. "I only told one little girl - around nine... ten? And she said she needed to know because of some dream... I don't know, she took the information and left."

Violet was enraged. She knew he was talking about Courtney, and her worst fear had come true. She knew about the undisclosed location.

"I'm sorry, I- I shouldn't have told anyone... But I have children at home, and I have to see them again - can you let me go? I'll do anything," pleaded the old man, tears forming in his eyes.

"Anything?" Violet asked, her eyebrows raised in suspicion. And when the old man nodded frantically, she saw an opportunity right before her eyes.

"I need you to find and bring me a crystal ball."

The old man looked at Violet, puzzled.

"A crystal ball? Is that it? If I get you any crystal ball, am I forgiven?" he asked, hopeful.

Violet threw her head back and laughed. "No, of course not. Nothing is that easy. I need the enchanted rose quartz crystal ball that belonged to the first Empress of Astria. They say it was her most prized possession. And soon enough, it will be mine... or else you're not going back home."

The old man whimpered but said nothing. Slowly, Violet untied the ropes binding him to the chair, and he stood up, trembling from head to toe.

"Remember, you screwed up, so you have to make up for it. Oh, and one more thing - the crystal ball hasn't been seen in centuries, so you'd better step up your game, off you go," she said, and he was gone.

***

Courtney woke up from the most comfortable sleep she'd had in weeks. Arthur had offered her the bed in the guest room of their cottage, as it was in good condition and was always empty.

She got dressed and walked out into the forest, where she agreed she'd meet Arthur at dawn. And, sure enough, he was sprawled lazily across a large rock, reading a book.

As soon as he saw Courtney, his face brightened and he gave her a warm smile. She returned it, and they began plotting their route for the day. They were to head up north into Floria, from where they would plan the rest of their journey, beginning the next day.

Arthur was a very entertaining person to travel with, and he had a lot of interesting stories to keep Courtney laughing the entire journey (which felt like it took just a few hours due to Arthur's company). And the closer the duo got to Floria, the closer Courtney felt to Arthur.

"Do your parents not mind you leaving so abruptly?"

That question was on Courtney's mind for quite some time, but she just said it casually as they were heading towards Floria. "Well, you see, my parents don't know what I do anymore... They passed away when I was six. I live with my grandmother now and she isn't exactly the type of grandmother who watches her grandchildren twenty-four hours a day, seven days a week. She thinks we're old and independent enough to take care of ourselves. She didn't even know I was leaving Lightley, and I'm pretty sure she won't notice either, as I usually spend most of my time in the forest of Astria," he said with a shrug, and neither of them mentioned the topic further.

They never ran out of things to talk about. When they stopped to eat, to rest, or to turn in for the night, the only thought on their minds was the journey the next day would bring. Unlike the search for the gate, the quest to the northern mountains of Astria was thrilling and exciting.

- Chapter 20 -

Excuses

Mrs. Carter had to make up multiple excuses to make up for both her daughters' absences. Courtney left 'for Katie's place' to spend the night, but that night turned into multiple nights. Unbeknownst to Courtney, Mrs. Carter did in fact know where she was and what she was doing. Amelia, on the other hand, had a valid reason to be out of the house. Right before her departure, she had written a note for her mother and left it behind, and the following morning, Mrs. Carter found it.

It read...

Mum,

The matter of Courtney's abrupt disappearance has concerned me greatly, and I felt the need to do something about it. By the time you read this, I will be out searching for her. I don't know when I will return, but, hopefully, I will return soon with Courtney by my side. I apologise for such short notice, and I hope you're not too upset with me.

-Amelia

Mrs. Carter was worried about her daughters, but she knew they were both worthy and brave enough to complete whatever task they set their minds to. So as soon as she read Amelia's note, she felt like the proudest mother in the world. Her daughters were growing up so fast... she could barely catch up with them. Her biggest fear was that one day they wouldn't need her, and they would be independent enough to live by their own advice. She felt ashamed of even having such thoughts, but it was a feeling she couldn't suppress. And now that both her daughters weren't home, all the emotion she had subdued came pouring out.

She was devastated after the loss of her husband, twelve years ago that very day. She prayed her daughters were fine... she couldn't afford to lose them, too.

And then came the slightly more complicated bit...

School was starting in two days, and Mrs. Carter had to make up a bunch of excuses to make up for Amelia's and Courtney's mysterious disappearances.

She felt guilty about lying to the teachers at school, especially since they were all incredibly considerate and cared about (and maybe even favourited) Amelia and Courtney. Maybe all except the history teacher.

But to Mrs. Carter, her children came first. They always did. So that night, she came up with a list of excuses to use when the unanswerable questions began rolling in. And, just in case, she hid Amelia's note in her drawer. She knew she was incredibly blessed to have such smart and independent daughters. It was just a matter of time until they came back, safe and strong, and made their mother even more proud than she already was. But there was a possibility that Courtney wouldn't... she could do much greater things outside the four walls of her flat.

- Chapter 21 -

Physically. Mentally? Never.

Amelia was situated up against a large rock, her arms and legs full of bleeding cuts. Her chest was rising and falling with every breath she took. She was as still as the forest surrounding her. Her hair was messy and untied, her eyelids shut over her brown eyes. The leather boots she had worn were all torn up and abandoned next to her stained backpack. She was exhausted to the point where she wouldn't wake up even if a foghorn sounded beside her ear. She had no idea where Courtney was, but she was ready to search the whole city for her sister. And since that was her goal from the very beginning, she stuck to it and was leaning against a boulder in one of the darkest forests in the city they resided in, her legs scarred from thorny bushes and her arms all cut due to swinging vines, fast asleep.

Every part of her ached, from top to toe. And she didn't mind having to go through that and more, as she thought that it was nothing compared to what her mother would be feeling at the moment, both her daughters missing, one of them without leaving a trace.

Amelia was in a deep-sleep, and the forest around her was asleep when she sat down against her boulder. However, with the sun rose numerous animals and insects, chirping, singing, and chittering merrily. It was hard for Amelia to sleep through all that, so she awoke, put her torn-up boots back on, and lifted her backpack to carry on her shoulders, but one of the straps snagged on a tree root sticking out from beneath the ground, and it was completely ripped off.

She sighed and swung the remaining strap over her shoulder. "Oh Courtney," she whispered, "where are you?"

"Are - we - there- yet?" panted Courtney, clutching a stitch in her side and trying not to collapse on the floor in a heap of sheer exhaustion.

"No - almost there - almost - there," replied Arthur, equally worn out. They were hiking across the uneven grounds of Roseview, heading north towards the mountains of Astria.

Roseview was located at the very top of Astria, and, according to every map Courtney and Arthur had purchased, was the last area to the north in all of Astria. And if there were no mountains ahead... then there was no hope left for Courtney.

Besides, Courtney already wasn't too hopeful about finding the mountains, as, according to what she knew about mountains, they were supposed to be cold... and, at the moment, she couldn't believe that there was a range of mountains to the north of where they currently were - sweat was running freely down her back and her face could easily be compared to a sun-ripened tomato due to the heat.

Arthur, however, was never discouraged. He kept motivating Courtney the entire way, occasionally making a joke or two when she looked like she needed it the most. Courtney was truly grateful he hadn't listened to her when she insisted he didn't accompany her, and her guilt quickly turned into gratitude.

She was learning more and more about Arthur, Astria, and magic. Her search for the Northern Mountains couldn't be more different from her search for the gate, like Astria, couldn't be more different from home. The sights were truly intriguing in Aurora Village, Exotica, and Lightley... trees were shrinking and growing rapidly, fairies were fluttering in groups or clusters, and the air seemed to shimmer in a mysterious, natural way. However, the same thing could not be said about Roseview. Despite the name, not a single plant, alive or dead, was to be seen, just miles and miles of sand in all directions. It was quite clear that this wasn't a frequently visited area of Astria.

They walked on for hours, then took a short break. Courtney collapsed on the sand, breathing heavily, Arthur beside her.

"Almost there," Courtney said in between steadying breaths. And this time, she believed it. She was so close to finding the mountains, finding the Empress, finding answers.

She remained lying motionless on the ground until a piece of paper flying with the wind caught her attention. As if her exhaustion had evaporated into thin air, she bolted towards the piece of paper, determined to catch it. She didn't know why she wanted it; she just did.

"Wait!" Arthur yelled, too tired to follow her. "Courtney! Where are you going?"

But Courtney was too busy to listen. She was running after the paper, the wind carrying it away, running through her hair, cooling her down. Finally, she caught it - the paper clenched tightly in her fist, she ran back to where she was lying on the ground moments ago, and started to read aloud,

Empress Tulip is now with me. We're in an old hut in the Northern Mountains. Nobody will find us there. Tulip doesn't have much power and magic left... It's happening now. She admits it herself. The throne will soon be occupied by someone truly worthy of it soon enough.

V.

Courtney felt like an iron fist was clenching her stomach. 'Tulip doesn't have much power and magic left... It's happening now.' What did that mean? Surely not... Empress Tulip was known for being incredibly powerful, she can take care of herself.

But that wasn't what made Courtney uneasy. It was the signature.

The old man mentioned that the only person who knew the location of Empress Tulip besides him and the Empress herself was... Violet. Who else could V. be?

But Courtney didn't want to believe it. She was convinced that Violet was trying to help save the Empress - and it hurt to find out the truth.

With all that was going on, Courtney completely forgot about Arthur's presence. So when he asked, "Are you okay?" concerned, she jumped and turned around.

"I- yes - no - I don't know," she sighed, "I thought Violet was trying to help - and I've been wrong all along."

Arthur didn't know how to respond for a while, but he then said, "It's alright. I'll help you locate the Empress. We'll find a way to bring her back to Pearl Palace. You needn't worry."

But apparently, that wasn't the best thing to say at the moment, for Courtney had lost it.

"No, Arthur! It doesn't work like that! There's no way I can help Empress Tulip with Violet seeking the throne! I'm no match for a fully grown magic practitioner!" she screamed. However, after she calmed down, Arthur was able to convince her that trying was better than nothing.

So they stood up and continued heading north, with nothing but billowing sand ahead. They had lunch on the go and didn't stop until they saw something - anything - other than sand in front of them.

And they didn't walk for that long before they needed to stop.

- Chapter 22 -

Awaiting Your Arrival

Strong, harsh winds howled outside, making the windows of Violet's hut rattle threateningly as if they were about to shatter any minute. A loud knock on the door could be heard, but barely. So when the sound of rapping on wood filled the room, Violet strode to the door and opened it, already expecting a visitor.

"Come in," she said to the old man, and he stepped inside the miserable hut. Violet gestured to an armchair opposite her own, and the man took a seat.

"So," she said, rubbing her hands together to keep warm. "Have you got it for real this time? I did tell you that this was your last chance the last time we met. Intrigue me," she reminded him, inclining her head towards a shelf filled with orbs, globes, and clear spheres. "Every time you come, you bring with you a crystal ball. And every time, it is never the one I ask you for. This is your last chance - do you have the quartz crystal ball?"

The old man nodded and pulled out a smooth, pink, glossy sphere with a golden base from beneath his cloak. He knew he had done a fine job, because as soon as Violet saw it, her eyes grew to twice their normal size and her hand twitched, eager to touch it.

"How did you - I know I asked, but I really didn't expect - very well... you shall leave. Go back home to your children, and stay away from here," she said, her hands still twitching and her eyes as big as saucers.

The old man bowed, kissed her hand, and left with a swish of his long black cloak, closing the door behind him. As soon as he left, Violet immediately dropped to her knees beside the table, her eyes drawn to the enchanted rose quartz crystal ball that once belonged to the first-ever Queen of Astria, and the only thing standing in the way between her and all the secrets the future holds.

She was opening her mind, slowly relaxing, adjusting to the feeling of crystal-gazing once more... It had been years since she had last used one of these beauties. However, as soon as she truly felt connected to the art of crystal gazing, and visions of the future began flowing freely into her mind, she was distracted.

An alarm sounded in her hut, and, astonished, she snapped her fingers, and the sound was gone. She sat back down and tried once more to gaze into the depths of the future, more determined than ever. And, a few minutes later, her nose was inches from the crystal, her eyes glossy, and her expression dazed as if she were in a trance.

Images from the future began flashing before her eyes but before she could get a good look at them, they were gone. But she caught glimpses of Pearl Palace, of the jewel-adorned quartz throne, and of the person sitting on it... and it wasn't Empress Tulip.

Violet smiled, cleared the shelf of all the worthless glass spheres, and placed her most valuable possession on it instead. Then she sat back, awaiting another visitor.

After what seemed like an endless amount of walking, Courtney and Arthur saw something that wasn't sand ahead. The dry land disappeared, and so did the sky. The only thing in front of them was... nothing. Just a blank, white space, like a vacuum.

They looked at each other, both with identical smiles, and nodded. They moved forward through the white space - or, at least, Courtney did. She walked through it and vanished from sight, while Arthur, on the other hand, slammed into an invisible barrier, which prevented him from passing through.

Then Courtney's head poked back through the barrier. "Come on, what are you waiting for? The Empress won't find herself," she said.

"I can't, something's preventing me from going through," he said, rubbing his head where it hit the barrier.

Courtney walked into Roseview and back again. Then she stuck her head out once more and shrugged. "It works for me," she muttered, puzzled but then it hit her, this barrier could be similar to the idea of the gate; 'only those with magic in their blood can enter the majestic lands that lay beyond it.' But then that meant Courtney had magic in her blood. The discovery frightened and intrigued her at the same time.

But Arthur was born in Astria... he had to be magical. It must have been something else that prevented him from crossing the barrier. But whatever it was, it was wasting their time so, for the final time, Courtney stepped back into Roseview.

"Arthur, you've helped me so much... and I couldn't be more grateful. But I think I was meant to do this alone - that's why you couldn't go through. Go back home, and stay safe, take this with you, I won't need it anymore," she handed him the complete map of Astria. "And don't worry about me, I'll be fine," she added, for Arthur had opened his mouth as if to protest.

"Alright," he said, "good luck."

After exchanging small smiles and a final look behind him, Arthur was slowly getting smaller and smaller as he walked away until Courtney could no longer see him, only sand in front of her and an empty stretch behind her.

- Chapter 23 -

Answers

Courtney kept walking through the endless blank
space - but she had no idea how, as there was no
visible floor beneath her feet. A few long minutes
later, she felt an icy frost tickle her spine, and the
tips of her fingers to the top of her toes began to
shiver. She knew she was close, and that excited
her, but she wished she had packed a winter
coat. She then began to feel snowflakes brushing
gently against her face, and the horizon ahead
slowly morphed from blank nothingness to
distant mountains capped with a thick layer of
snow. She smiled a weak smile, her teeth
chattering uncontrollably now, and she ran as
fast as she could, eager to reach the mountains,
amazed at her huge accomplishment, and charged

with adrenaline. She only stopped to take a break when her legs were too weak to carry on walking from malnutrition. She sat down, took out a snack, and rested her back against a tree trunk. She wished she could get warmer...

And as soon as that thought crossed her mind, a fire sprung up in front of her, crackling and melting the snow around it. Courtney gaped, open-mouthed, at what she had unintentionally produced. She finished her food, warmed up a little beside the fire before extinguishing it with a handful of snow, and continued walking until she had reached the base of the foremost mountain which, she noticed when she craned her neck up, had a withered-looking cabin built dangerously high atop it.

Courtney placed her backpack at the base of the mountain. She figured that was the 'old hut' mentioned in Violet's letter, and she kept her eyes on it as she slowly but steadily began making her way up the mountain. The higher she went, the colder she got, but that didn't make her give up.

"Don't look down," she kept muttering under her breath. "You can do this."

Her fingers were full of blisters and her legs were full of cuts, not to mention that her whole body was shivering violently. But she was incredibly perseverant, and, with immense difficulty, Courtney was able to hoist herself onto a flat surface large enough for her to place her whole foot on, from where she had to leap in order to reach the hut. It was a big leap, and Courtney was jittery as she attempted to jump toward it, but she lost her balance and nearly slipped.

With steadying breaths, Courtney tried again. She felt the sensation of falling... she wasn't going to make it... but her hand was able to grip a part of the mountain and slowly pull herself up. Breathless, she emerged on a lopsided surface between two mountains where the hut lay, its door slightly ajar.

She pushed the door open with her sore fingertips and peeked inside. It was pitch-black. With bated breath, she stepped inside and tried to feel her way around the hut. And then a faint torchlight illuminated a pale face with long, thick eyelashes.

It was Violet.

"Hello, Courtney," she said with a smile, "glad you could make it."

"You!" Courtney yelled furiously. She had stopped shivering, and both her fists were clenched on either side of her body.

Violet only replied with a smile. Courtney then realised that there was another person in the room. She ran towards a little bed draped with lacy sheets - and on which Empress Tulip lay. Frantic, Courtney began smoothening her sheets, suppressing a tear.

"She's not dead," came a soft voice from behind her. She wheeled around to find Violet, placing a hand on Courtney's shoulder. Courtney pushed it off.

"It's just a temporary sleeping enchantment," Violet said airily and waved her hand in the air. The Empress' eyes immediately fluttered open and crinkled into a kind smile.

"See?"

But Courtney wasn't convinced. "Why is she here, and not in Pearl Palace, doing her job? Why did you keep her here?" she said, wishing Violet had a reasonable answer to her question, wishing she had been wrong to doubt her.

"It's quite a long story, why don't you take a seat?" Violet said with a half-smile, gesturing towards the empty high-backed armchair opposite her own.

Courtney had forgotten how much her legs ached and how numb her feet felt until that moment. The Empress sat up in her bed with difficulty.

"It all started when you began getting strange dreams. Dreams you couldn't quite explain. Those dreams weren't normal and you sensed it.

You had a fiery determination to achieve what you heard because you were doing it for the benefit of others, and not out of greed," Violet started, "you had a tenacity unlike any other I've ever seen. It's outstanding how a thirteen-year-old like yourself could achieve such wondrous things. However, it wasn't just your determination I would like to praise, but your bravery as well. You have overcome many barriers that led you to where you are right now," she continued.

Courtney wished she would move on and say something she didn't know already but she remained silent.

"You have achieved what you set out to do, making me and many others proud. You found the gate, opened it, and that..." she said softly with a smile, "is where I come in. You see, there were rumours that you would arrive in Astria one day, and I believed them to be rumours and rumours only... until you indeed arrived. I listened to your story and remembered what people used to say about you. You see, not everyone could step foot in Astria. The gate you located is invisible to anyone who doesn't have magic in their blood, and the border to the mountains of Astria can only be penetrated by people of magical backgrounds. But when I knew your name, and I remembered hearing about the same dream you had many years ago, I knew you were destined to be here all along."

Courtney was confused. "What does my name and my dream have to do with anything?"

"Your last name, you're a Carter!"

It was the first time Empress Tulip spoke up. Courtney had almost forgotten about her presence in the room.

"What difference does that make?" Violet and Empress Tulip exchanged smiles then turned to face Courtney.

"Because," said the Empress, "My full name is Tulip Elizabeth Carter."

Courtney gaped at the Empress, unable to believe what she had just heard.

"You're my ancestor?" she asked in disbelief, expecting to be told this was all a big joke and that magic never existed in the first place, but wishing with all her heart that what the Empress said was true.

"Your great-great-great-grandmother from your father's side," Empress Tulip replied with a wink. Courtney did notice that their dazzling blue eyes were quite similar.

But that led to more confusion.

"Why, though, was I expected to arrive in Astria? Why did I get those dreams that led me here? Are my friends and family safe?" Courtney asked.

This was too much information and she was trying to wrap her head around it all. Empress Tulip's smile didn't vanish, but Courtney felt it falter slightly.

"You will know, my dear. But first, let Violet

explain," said Empress Tulip.

Violet handed Courtney a cup of warm tea and a slice of fruitcake, and then she sat down in her armchair, hands folded in her lap. "Make yourself comfortable. It's a long story," she said.

Courtney relaxed her tensed muscles and sipped quietly at her tea. It warmed her down to her fingertips. Despite the cushiony armchair, sugary fruitcake, and warm tea, she wasn't feeling comfortable and wished Violet would get to the point before her patience ran out.

"I immediately took you to Pearl Palace," Violet continued, "but I had forgotten that our Empress Tulip, wise and powerful..." she gave a polite nod towards the Empress, which she returned, "...had the ability to see past the borders of Astria, so it was quite a shock to me as it was to you when we discovered her absence in the Palace. However, when we arrived, the note she had left behind explained that she was aware of your arrival here, and knew that you were a true

Carter. You both have the same liking for mischief, and the same perseverance in tough situations. She hid up here in the Northern Mountains, waiting for you to find your way here and prove yourself worthy. I must admit, though," she said, her eyebrows raised, "I didn't expect you to find your way. But Empress Tulip had faith in you. She felt you could do it, and here you are now!" She finished, wearing a bright smile identical to the one she was wearing when she introduced herself to Courtney for the first time.

Courtney still felt like there was a missing piece to the puzzle. "I'm here now. I came to help save the Empress. But she's been here willingly the whole time... and you've been expecting me to be here," she said.

After saying it, it sounded even more befuddling and then it hit her: the note. Her face turned a nasty green and her stomach churned as she completely lost her appetite, setting her teacup down on the table with a soft clunk.

"It can't be..." she whispered to herself, but she knew that it was, and she couldn't change that. Why else would she be there?

She walked over and sat on the edge of Empress Tulip's bed.

"I won't last forever. I want you to be the new Empress of Astria. Just promise me you will take care of it when I'm gone. Do you accept?" The Empress asked with tears in her eyes.

Behind her, Violet gave a small sob.

Courtney couldn't believe it. "M-me? An Empress? Why not my mother, she's more skilled, or my sister Amelia, she's incredibly clever. Why me?"

The Empress wiped her tears on the back of her sleeve and smiled. "Because you, my dear, are creative, far more than any other person in this family, and that's exactly what Astria needs. A strong, independent, and creative ruler. Not to mention your need to ensure that people around you are safe. That is what brought you here in the first place, wasn't it? And proof of that is your dreams. I had those dreams when I was your age. And you were the first person after me to receive them. Are you convinced now?"

Courtney gave a weak smile and nodded. "I promise," she whispered solemnly. She was willing to stick to her promise and make her family proud.

- Chapter 24 -

Solitude

Arthur kicked a small pebble and chased it down a steep hill, never averting his eyes from it while it rolled down the uneven dirt. He was in a sulky mood because of what happened with Courtney earlier. He knew she was capable enough of completing the journey herself, but he wished he could still have been there to help and accompany her. Because for once, he was having fun with other people, and it was raising his spirits far more than isolation did. And now, he was going back to a quiet life with his boastful brothers and elderly grandmother, and long, lonely strolls around the forest of Astria. Which he didn't really mind. He had lived in peace for nine years that way. It was just that... he preferred being with Courtney.

He took occasional glances at the map she passed him and continued heading back south. He wondered if Courtney found the old hut yet. He sighed. Even if she did, he wouldn't know. It was such a short time they had spent together, but Arthur felt like he had known her his entire life. He just hoped Courtney wouldn't forget him when she became famous for being the Empress's rescuer or something heroic like that. The thought made the corners of his mouth form a sad, small smile. He could already imagine her stuttering and stumbling over her words when people crowded around her to ask how many magical monarchs she had rescued from evil fairies while she was trying to explain that she was not aware of Astria's existence up until last month.

He laughed and checked the map once more. He was heading too far west. Once Arthur corrected his route, he let his imagination take hold of him once more. He thought of his brothers, too busy to acknowledge his existence, and what they might think when he told them that he was off with a thirteen-year-old girl who also happened to be on a self-set mission to rescue Astria's beloved Empress Tulip. They'd probably think he was having weird dreams, or trying to gain attention. As usual.

He thought of his grandmother and how she would whisper not-so-quietly (so that his brothers could hear) that Arthur was her favourite. How she had willingly taken care of three growing boys when their parents died. How she had stayed strong for her grandchildren, only for them to leave her and go their separate ways. Arthur realised that they had been using her for her resources and shelter... and the rest they did for themselves.

If he couldn't find a way to go back and help Courtney, he decided to spend as much time with his grandmother as he possibly could - she didn't deserve solitude.

"Ashton, Julia."

"Present."

"Atkins, Theodore."

"Present."

"Blackwell, Judy."

Silence.

"Blythe, Harry."

"Present."

"Cameron, James."

"Present."

"Carter - Clover, Katie."

As the register was being taken during form class, Katie's mind was not with her teacher, but somewhere else completely.

Theodore Atkins, the boy who sat beside her, gave her a slight nudge to indicate that the teacher had announced her name.

"Present!" she had called just as the teacher was about to call the next name. The seat on her left-hand side was occupied by Theodore, but the seat on her right was empty.

"Courtney," she whispered silently, "are you alright? Did you find your gate?"

"Who are you talking to?" asked Theodore, his eyebrow raised in suspicion.

Katie bit her lip, furious with herself for being so careless.

"N-nobody," she stuttered.

"Quiet, you two, while I do the register," snapped the teacher.

Unconvinced, Theodore turned his seat back to its original position. Katie exhaled, relieved. She had promised Courtney that she wouldn't mention her mission to anyone. And this was a close call.

She stuck a small note beneath what used to be Courtney's desk, where it joined multiple other notes that Katie had written for Courtney. It felt just like exchanging notes during class, except that she wasn't receiving a note back. It just wasn't the same without her best friend by her side.

- Chapter 25 -

Welcome Back

Violet clapped her hands once, and all the possessions around the cottage zoomed into a circular suitcase that lay open on the floor. Courtney glimpsed a pale pink spherical object. Violet clapped again, two short claps this time, and the suitcase zipped itself up and flew into her outstretched hand. She bewitched it so that it was feather-light. Empress Tulip smiled at Courtney.

"Ready to go back to Pearl Palace?" she asked.

Courtney nodded.

Violet led the Empress out of her bed and walked her to the door. She pulled a handful of shimmering powder from one of her coat pockets and sprinkled it over the three of them. Immediately, they were teleported to the base of the mountain where there was nothing but a blank stretch of snow-covered land lay a powder-blue prestigious carriage into which Violet tossed the suitcase and helped Empress Tulip into, and Courtney followed her inside. Violet squeezed in beside them. The Empress raised her hand and brought it down swiftly. The carriage around them disappeared - and so did they. Once more, there was nothing but snow and mountains around them with the cabin, peeking through two mountaintops far behind them.

"Can't be seen right now," Violet muttered, while the wheels of the invisible carriage trundled as the snow beneath them crunched. She muttered something inaudible under her breath and their tracks disappeared from behind them.

The journey back was much more enjoyable than the journey to the Northern Mountains of Astria. Courtney was able to enjoy the scenery in a luxurious carriage which, she realised, drove itself. All that was missing was Arthur's company. Courtney removed the thought from her mind. Arthur was home safe now, no longer in constant danger because of her. Each was where she felt they belonged.

They passed many places and people, but nobody saw them. Whenever they needed food or water, Violet would disguise herself as a villager and get them something to eat.

Two days later, they arrived at the marvellous pearly doors of Pearl Palace. Stiff and exhausted, the three of them piled out of the carriage and entered the palace, fully visible.

As soon as the door opened and people glimpsed who was behind them, a crowd of fairies swarmed around Empress Tulip and Courtney but Violet held up her hand. "Make space, please," she said, her voice hinting how tired she was.

There was a scramble around the room as people scuttled around to make way for the Empress, Violet, and Courtney. They nodded politely and climbed the shimmering staircase of clouds. Empress Tulip led Courtney and Violet into her office and sat them down. She stroked the arm of her throne before sitting herself down.

"Courtney," she said, giving her a piercing look with her signature blue eyes, "you have achieved inconceivable things, and you have proven yourself worthy of the title of Empress. You might get the role earlier than expected. Because of that, your coronation will take place tomorrow. Sorry for such abrupt news and short notice, but it's for the best. After that, Violet will help you learn to enhance and control your magic. You have great opportunities ahead of you, and at such a young age, you have sufficient of time to make this a better place. Make us proud. For now, go get some rest. You've earned it," she winked at Courtney.

Courtney nodded and headed towards her room. She fell asleep as soon as her head hit the pillow, still in her day clothes.

- Chapter 26 -

See You

The next day, Courtney woke up early, put on her periwinkle-coloured dress, and styled her hair into a neat bun. She slipped her feet into a pair of silver slippers and made her way down the corridor and to Empress Tulip's office as they had arranged. She knocked twice.

"Come in," said a cheerful voice from behind the wooden door. Courtney gently pushed the door open and stepped inside, closing it again behind her.

Empress Tulip sat on her throne, a wide smile on her face. "Good morning! Nice to see you up so bright and early," she said.

Courtney didn't reply, so Empress Tulip continued, "You look fantastic. Would you like to have breakfast downstairs? The coronation doesn't begin until one!"

Courtney nodded, and they both went down to the dining hall. The time Courtney saw it before didn't count as a proper dinner. Then, all the fairies kept mostly to themselves, tension filled the air and Violet and Empress Tulip were not present at the time.

Now it was a completely different scene. Fairies were having open discussions, the atmosphere was incredibly bright and cheery and the tables were laden with scrambled eggs, pancakes, french toast, bagels, quiches, and much more. Smiling faces illuminated the room.

The Empress sat in her usual seat at the end of the table and requested Courtney sit on the chair beside her. Many people smiled at her, but nobody asked questions. Violet must have warned them. Everybody seemed overjoyed to have their Empress back.

Empress Tulip, herself, was feeling much more cheerful and energetic now that she was back where she belonged.

Breakfast in Pearl Palace was a delightful affair. As soon as Courtney finished eating, she dashed back upstairs to have a quick second in her bedroom while coronation preparations were being made.

She looked at herself in the mirror, let her flowing curls down, and changed into her elaborate lilac gown adorned with rhinestones. She kept her silver slippers on.

A gentle knock sounded on her door, and Violet's head peeked inside.

"Are we starting early?" Courtney asked her, but Violet shook her head.

"There are some people here to see you," she said. "Come down when you're ready."

See her? Who would come here to see her? Courtney ran, unable to wait and rushed downstairs, unable to wait. Violet was startled at the sudden change of energy, but she smiled.

Courtney had to remind herself to slow down, and she descended slowly, careful not to skip any steps, although when she saw who was standing in front of the gates, she couldn't help but run.

"Mum? Amelia? You're here?" Courtney squealed.

Mrs. Carter and Amelia stood in front of the pearly white gates, wearing identical smiles and looking around in awe.

"Courtney," her mom said, her eyes welling with tears. "I've missed you."

She held her daughter close and hugged her tightly. When Mrs. Carter released Courtney from her tight embrace, Amelia took her sister's hands into her own. "You look stunning," she whispered. "Wait-" Amelia said, taking out her diamond teardrop earrings and putting them on Courtney's ears.

"Now you do," she said with a grin.

"Thanks, big sis," laughed Courtney, "how'd the science competition go?"

"Oh my god, I'd forgotten about that. I did it! I made it to the final!" she beamed. But not as brightly as Courtney, who hugged her and whispered in her ear, "I knew it."

"You also have another guest," said Mrs. Carter, her eyebrows raised.

A shy, grinning head appeared in the crack between the gates. "Arthur!" Courtney yelled with glee. "You're here!"

"Of course I'm here," he said, smiling. I wouldn't miss your coronation!"

Courtney chuckled. "Have some breakfast," she said to her mother, Amelia, and Arthur. "I'm coming."

- Chapter 27 -

The Coronation

Courtney met Empress Tulip at the top of the shimmering staircase at twelve fifty-five.

"Are you ready?" the Empress asked.

Courtney nodded, smiling. They walked downstairs to the Grand Hall, which was decorated for the occasion. As soon as they reached, thunderous applause broke out across the room.

Empress Tulip's throne was moved to the middle of the hall for everyone to see, and an identical chair made from quartz and velvet was placed beside it for Courtney. The council of Astria was seated behind them. A small, round table was placed between the thrones, and it held the crown in a glass case.

What looked like all of Astria was standing in the Grand Hall, each individual trying to get a closer look at the crown. Courtney and Empress Tulip took a seat, and Courtney was officially crowned the next Empress of Astria, and subsequently presented with the crown and a rose quartz crystal ball.

After that, people mingled, conversed, and reunited in the Grand Hall and Courtney spent all day with her family, with Arthur, and with the people she loved. She wished she could tell Katie all this.

And that was when she realised that she could. The gate was concealed from mankind for decades but what if the magical and the non-magical community mixed together? What if Astria was open to the rest of the world?

She didn't share that thought with anyone, but she did keep it in mind. That occasion was an important highlight in the history of Astria, and it wasn't to be soon forgotten. Courtney was the youngest person to ever be crowned Empress of Astria, and she had plans. Plans to make it a much better place, and to change the world as we know it today.

As if on cue, the day after Courtney's coronation, Courtney and Violet were seated beside Empress Tulip's occupied bed. Her magic was running out, and she didn't have long to live. The Council of Astria - which consisted of four fairies: Holly, Daniel, Alex, and Nicola - were seated at the foot of the bed.

There was not a dry eye in the room.

Nobody wanted to move or leave Empress Tulip, even when the white light signalling the start of lunchtime flashed repeatedly. They only moved when the Empress requested to talk to Courtney, alone.

One by one, they stood up and left the room, leaving just Courtney seated by the bed of Empress Tulip.

"Courtney. I cannot explain how proud I am of you. I may have only met you two days ago, but I feel like I've known you for years. I cannot reiterate how selfless you were when making several contributions for the sake of the community. You will make an exceptional Empress. Don't worry, if you ever feel lost, unsure, or doubtful, remember what you have accomplished. Make Astria proud, make me proud," she smiled, and then she stopped breathing, her heart stopped beating and her blue eyes were empty and lifeless.

She was gone.

- Chapter 28 -

Permanent Changes

After Empress Tulip's passing, a council meeting was held, which Courtney was required to join. The Council was mainly preparing Courtney for taking Empress Tulip's job and asking her for suggestions to see her point of view, as they were told by Violet that she was very creative and had unique points of view on various matters. She did have one suggestion, but she wasn't sure the Council of Astria would approve. It seemed far-fetched and ridiculous.

But she said it anyway.

"I do have one suggestion... and it's the riddance of the gate that separates Astria from the rest of the world. What is the point of keeping magical people away from non-magical areas, and vice versa? We are all different - unique - and getting rid of the gate would be the first step to embrace that."

Silence followed her suggestion, and she wondered if she had said the right thing. To her surprise, the members of the council broke out in applause for her.

"Violet was right. You do have a wide imagination," Holly said, "however, I'm not sure the rest of Astria would approve."

Alex interjected. "But Courtney is The Empress. Even if they don't agree with her, Courtney's decision is final. And, besides," he said smiling at Courtney, "who knows? Maybe they'll change their minds, or even offer to help with the project."

And everyone seemed to agree on that, so the following day, a group of knights set off to take down the gate, led by Sir William. Courtney stood on the balcony of her new office, looking across the lands that were now under her law.

She smiled, telling herself that she wouldn't let her people down. She walked inside and sat on her throne, pulling out a book to read and pass the time. She was soon joined by her sister, who casually strolled into the room as if it was her own.

"Amelia, you know there's such a thing as knocking," Courtney said matter-of-factly, flipping a page. Amelia ignored her.

"I just want to say... I'm proud of you, Courtney. I know I don't say this often, and I know that we don't spend as much time together as we used to, but you'll always be close to my heart," she said.

Courtney was surprised by the unexpected gesture, but she was touched nonetheless. The truth was, she felt the same way. "Thanks, Amelia, you'll always be close to my heart, too."

The next day, Sir William and his men were back at the palace, carrying a large, rotting wooden board. The gate.

"Shall we dispose of this, Your Highness?" Sir William asked.

"One second," Courtney said and broke a small piece of it that was covered in moss and pocketed it. "Yes, you may dispose of it now," she said. The gates were officially opened: It was time for a permanent change.

The End

About the Author

Talia Arabiat

At the age of eleven years old, Talia, now twelve, penned her story, setting the stage for her flourishing writing career. As her favourite school subject, English is not just a school subject for her; it's a passion that fuels her creativity and imagination.

When she's not lost in the pages of a book, you'll find her crafting her own stories, scripts, and poetry, each word a testament to her enthusiasm for storytelling. In her spare time, Talia enjoys reading, writing, shopping and exploring new places.

Talia's interests extend beyond the realm of literature, with a passion for both the creative and the practical, she envisions a career in architecture and interior design, where she can blend her love for aesthetics with her talent for spatial design.

Amidst her professional pursuits, Talia aims to dabble as a hobbyist author, sharing her imaginative tales with the world, and infusing each word with a message of positivity, creativity, and kindness. It's not just about her own stories, though; she strives to be a role model for aspiring writers, encouraging them to share their own unique pieces of literature and spread their voices far and wide.

Follow Talia's publishing journey here,

www.youngauthoracademy.com/talia

[scan with your device]

Printed in Great Britain
by Amazon